# THE CAT BETWEEN

ALSO BY LOUISE CARSON

NOVELS

*The Cat Vanishes*

*The Cat Among Us*

*Executor*

*In Which: Book One of The Chronicles of Deasil Widdy*

*Measured: Book Two of The Chronicles of Deasil Widdy*

NOVELLA

*Mermaid Road*

POETRY

*A Clearing*

*Rope: A Tale Told in Prose and Verse*

# THE CAT BETWEEN

A MAPLES MYSTERY

LOUISE CARSON



DOUG WHITEWAY, EDITOR

Signature
EDITIONS

Cover design by Doowah Design.
Cover icons: The Noun Project and Doowah Design.

This book was printed on Ancient Forest Friendly paper.
Printed and bound in Canada by Hignell Book Printing Inc.

We acknowledge the support of the Canada Council for the Arts and the Manitoba Arts Council for our publishing program.

**Library and Archives Canada Cataloguing in Publication**

Title: The cat between / Louise Carson ; Doug Whiteway, editor.
Names: Carson, Louise, 1957- author.
| Whiteway, Doug, 1951- editor.
Description: Series statement: A Maples mystery
Identifiers: Canadiana (print) 20190177810
| Canadiana (ebook) 20190177829
| ISBN 9781773240497 (softcover) | ISBN 9781773240503 (HTML)
Classification: LCC PS8605.A7775 C383 2019
| DDC C813/.6—dc23

Signature Editions
P.O. Box 206, RPO Corydon, Winnipeg, Manitoba, R3M 3S7
www.signature-editions.com

*for Jackie O and Mata,*
*the latest arrivals*

CONTENTS

PART 1
WITCH'S BROOM
9

PART 2
SHRIKE
59

PART 3
FISHER
115

PART 4
COYWOLF
157

# PART 1

# WITCH'S BROOM

*The slim grey cat crouched in the snowy thicket between the house of many cats and the empty house next door.*

*Except the latter wasn't empty. At least not tonight. Tonight it hummed with activity both upstairs and down. Voices. Lights. Coloured lights at an upstairs window.*

*From where he sat, he saw through a window as two men entered a back room of the house on the ground floor. They both had small lights they flashed around the room. He crept a bit closer and jumped on a narrow ledge below one window. He made himself very still.*

*He heard two voices rise suddenly in argument. Then the men seemed to reach some agreement. He slowly raised his head. One man, dressed in a bulky one-piece garment, handed a cat-sized package to the other man. The second man was wearing what the cat recognized as clothes similar to what his owner—the old man—would wear: trousers under a long warm-looking coat, a scarf and a hat.*

*As he watched, the second man removed the hat and placed it on a counter next to a round black plastic object that reminded the cat of a fishbowl in the home of one of his previous owners. He remembered the fun he'd had scooping the little goldfish out of the water and watching them flop around before eating them. He had been charmed and waited hopefully for that owner to restock the bowl.*

*It hadn't happened. Instead, the next day, he was thrust into his cat carrier and returned to the cat adoption agency. "Just isn't working out," his then owner had snapped before stomping out.*

*The men's voices were raised again as they looked at the package's contents. The first man grabbed the fishbowl and put it on his head.*

*The cat blinked. Original. Fishbowl man left the second man rewrapping the package. Fishbowl slammed an invisible door. The second man sighed, put on his hat and also left the room.*

*The cat heard a car engine start and then, farther away down the road, a much louder motor roar into life. He waited a moment and dropped off the window ledge into the snow.*

*He was retreating back toward the thicket and his own comfortable home beyond the house of many cats when a new sound behind him made him turn. He looked up.*

*The glow of the different coloured lights upstairs was growing stronger. They must be strung together like the lights the neighbour women had recently hung around his old man's fireplace. These ones upstairs might be hung around the inside of the room's window. But the sound.*

*A little child stood in the open window, laughing. It held a cat in its arms. A black cat with white legs.*

*The grey cat stiffened. His secret name for himself was Defiance and all other cats were his enemies. He didn't know why. It was just the way he was made. His fur lifted on his back and his tail fluffed.*

*Strange. He could smell the cat but not the child. As he watched, the lights pulsed stronger and stronger as the child laughed and laughed.*

*Then—and it seemed as if it all happened at once—the cat fell, the window slammed down, and the lights went off.*

*He blinked. Where was the cat? He trotted forward towards the snow under the window.*

# 1

"Crazy weather, eh?" Gerry remarked idly to the young man standing next to her.

"How, crazy?" he replied in heavily accented English, a puzzled look on his face.

"Uh, it's very mild. Everything is melting." He must not be from around here, she thought, noting the olive skin and thick black hair. She looked around restlessly. Would this tour ever begin?

"Is spring, no?"

She laughed. He looked hurt. "No, no, I'm not laughing at you. No. Spring is three months away. In April. If we're lucky, I'm told. This mild weather is temporary." When he continued to look puzzled, she extrapolated. "Winter will return soon. Very cold. Lots of snow."

He nodded rather absently, then said, "So, animals will return to sleep."

She wondered what on earth he could be referring to, then remembered the squirrels that she'd noticed reappearing during this January thaw. She also nodded. "Yes, the hibernating ones are only out temporarily." He seemed to retreat into his own thoughts and to Gerry's relief the guide arrived. They set off around the campus.

Many of the buildings were linked, but they'd been told to dress for outdoors and, soon enough, were wading across a slushy road.

This building was new. Dedicated to science and technology, it gleamed. And it was a comfortable temperature. Students soon began unzipping jackets as their guide extolled the building's virtues.

Gerry could see her companion was interested. His dark eyes set in a thin face darted around. She looked at the others in the group. Mostly young, some nervous ones, some obviously foreign students or new immigrants.

She'd seen the orientation tour on the list of activities for the first week of term and thought it might be fun, or at least useful. As a last-minute substitute teacher, she had to get her bearings fast.

"Bloody hell!" the harried administrator had muttered as she'd rooted around her desk for Gerry's details. "You think you have everything organized—oh, here you are." She pulled Gerry's resumé out from under a course syllabus. "Jen Carstairs—that's who you're replacing, sort of—teaches this course—Bridging the Gap: Western Painting from Romanticism to the Twentieth Century—and she's very good. Well, she's almost due—her second—and lined up her replacement herself, a young artist who's visiting from France for a year." She looked at her desk calendar and jabbed a finger into the middle of January. "And what does he do? Last week he drives his Jeep into the side of a mountain." Gerry winced. "Oh, he'll be fine, but he's broken a lot of bones. Two months before he's even walking."

She cleared her throat and studied Gerry's list of accomplishments. "University of Toronto, fine arts, great honours; commercial artist; comic strip *Mug the Bug*. *Mug the Bug*! My kids love Mug!" She stretched a hand across the desk. "You've got the job. Tuesdays and Thursdays, one to three-thirty."

Gerry stopped daydreaming. Apparently they were done touring the science building and walking towards her new place of work—Gladys Berta Macdonald Hall, or Mac Hall, as the guide referred to it. He was speaking and this time Gerry paid attention as they stood in the entrance hall.

"This fine old building, built around the turn of the previous century, is in the neoclassical style. Note the columns and arched windows, the height of the ceilings; even some of the light fixtures are from 100 years ago."

I bet some of the dirt dates that far back too, Gerry thought wryly, looking up at the elaborate plasterwork around the dingy glass and metal lantern, its chain black with tarnish. And the heating system. No one on the tour opened their jackets here. She rested her hand on a radiator. Tepid. Must remember that and dress warmly.

She looked up at the painting of Gladys Berta Macdonald herself, a handsome woman with dark hair and eyes, in a white presentation gown complete with tiara and sash. How the times they have a'changed, thought Gerry. A local notable, she supposed; then heard the guide explain how Gladys Berta's family had donated the land for the college over 100 years earlier.

They were outside again, trudging behind their guide. He led them back to their starting place in the administration wing of the linked buildings. Humanities, police technology and physical education all resided here. Gerry spied a pool and made a note to check when she could use it.

She turned to the young foreign student to wish him well, but somewhere during the tour, he'd melted away. She shrugged and headed for her car, parked about as far as possible from the buildings.

A rural college, Ross Davidson had dedicated as much of its total area to parking lots as buildings, probably because most of its students arrived by car.

Gerry surveyed her red and white Austin Mini Cooper with satisfaction. It had sustained some damage when a tree crushed it during an ice storm on Christmas day, but the dealer had done a good job repairing it.

She rooted in her coat pocket for the parking decal she'd paid for and picked up that morning. She got in and stuck it on the upper left corner of the windshield. There, she thought, I'm legal. During the drive home, she tried not to worry about teaching her first college-level class the next day.

"Hello, cats. I'm home," she called out cheerily, letting herself in the kitchen entrance at the side of The Maples, the old family home she'd been living in for the last eight months after inheriting it (and the cats) from her Aunt Maggie.

There wasn't much response, but she heard a few thuds as furry bodies dropped to the floor in other parts of the house. She found the cats sluggish in this deepest part of winter and, far from driving her crazy from being cooped up (as she'd feared), they mostly just slept and ate.

Gerry closed the kitchen door, put on the kettle and prepared cat suppers. First she topped up the footbath-sized plastic tub of kibble on the floor under the tiny kitchen table. Then nineteen saucers were lined up and nineteen heaping tablespoons of tinned cat food were ladled out. She'd found it a stinky messy job at first but now could have done it in her sleep and, on certain mornings, did.

She put the saucers on the floor under the table, made her coffee and opened the door. The cats had assembled outside it as she worked, and jostled each other to find a dish. Gerry spared a moment to ensure Jay, the black and white kitten and newest member of the pride, wasn't bullied but needn't have bothered. Mother, a large marmalade tiger and Jay's adoptive parent, was on the job, protecting the little one as she ate.

Gerry passed into the living room and flopped in one of two rocking chairs in front of a cold grate. I should make a fire, she thought. Later. She held her warm mug in both hands and sipped. A double espresso with lots of milk and brown sugar. She exhaled. "Ah." Then she looked at the long table under a window that served as her workstation during winter and flinched.

*Mug the Bug*, her successful comic strip that ran daily in several newspapers, was only one week away from the disaster of running out of episodes. She liked to be two weeks ahead.

"Anybody have any ideas?" she asked the cats, some of whom, finished eating, had joined her by the hearth. A general consensus that grooming took precedence over brainstorming seemed to be her answer. She reached down and stroked the two closest to her feet.

"Hello, Cocoon. Hello, Max." The two cats in question, one a fluffy grey and white, the other a fluffy orange and white, paused in their post-prandial licking. "Oh, don't mind me," Gerry teased. They didn't and returned to the important task of keeping all that fur perfect.

Next to the pile of papers that was Mug, her prototype children's book—*The Cake-Jumping Cats of Dibble*—languished. There had been too much going on. The aftermath of the Christmas storm; having her part-time housekeeper Prudence Crick practically move in after her cottage took a tree through its roof; Gerry nursing Prudence through the flu; then them finding two bodies—one old and one new, and the subsequent fallout from that—had conspired to keep Gerry from doing what she loved—creating.

Another pile of papers included her family's genealogy and local history. She should put that away, she mused. It would distract her from the fourth pile, the one that loomed ominously in her immediate future—her notes for the art history course.

With a sigh, she realized she'd finished her coffee just as Bob, her black and white tuxedo cat, jumped into her lap. "Sorry, Bob. Your timing's off. But I'll make you a nice fire." She stood up and the cat slid onto the braided hearthrug. He looked at her reproachfully, stuck one hind leg up in the air and began the most personal of grooming rituals. "That tells me," murmured Gerry as she went about her chores.

An hour later, cat boxes cleaned, garbage tossed, wood supplies replenished and a fire crackling behind a screen, she sat down at her living room table. She quickly reviewed her notes for the first lecture—an overview of the whole period she was expected to cover, from the latter half of the nineteenth century to just before the First World War. When she thought she felt all right about that, she pulled *Mug the Bug* over.

Like Prudence, Mug was away on a Caribbean vacation. But Gerry had never been on such a trip and she was drawing a blank. She tried to remember what her friends Cece and Bea had told her about their recent trip to Jamaica. Pleasurable as lolling by the sea might be, it wasn't very funny, and humour was what Gerry was trying to manufacture.

She recalled they'd gone on a tour to a plantation where formerly rum had been made. She thought about Mug, an infinitely small speck on the page, sampling various rums, becoming inebriated, and then what? She tentatively sketched a few scenarios and when she had one that made her smile—Mug drunkenly singing while riding the plantation waterwheel as bemused tourists watched from below—was satisfied.

Since she'd gotten home, the sun had set, and when she lifted her head to look out the back window, the snow on the lawn had turned from white to blue, the trees across the lake from dark green to black. She thought she saw something flutter in a tree by the shore and then her growling stomach made her look away and ask, "Well, what's for my supper, cats?"

After her baked beans and toast, a cup of tea and some cookies, all consumed at the table among her projects, Gerry had managed another episode for Mug and retired to her bed.

As she drifted off—Bob cuddled close and a tortoiseshell named Lightning nestled by her feet—she thought she heard a lonely howl far away.

# 2

B*ring, bring. Bring, bring.*

From a dream where she was afloat in her own backyard swimming pool as her cats took running dives to join her, Gerry swam back up to consciousness. She opened one eye. Her radio alarm clock reposed peacefully on her bedside table. A digital 6:15 slid to 6:16. *Bring, bring.* Her phone? At this time of the morning?

Dragging on her robe and slippers, she flumped downstairs to the kitchen. Maybe an extension in the upstairs office would be a good idea. She picked up the phone. "Hello?" she groggily inquired, then quickly snapped to attention.

"Yes, Blaise. Missing? Since sometime in the night? Yes, of course. I'll be right over." She ran upstairs, hurried into her clothes and returned to the kitchen, shrugging on her coat and grabbing her keys. On the little kitchen porch she stepped into the giant all-purpose boots Prudence had recommended she buy. She could hear Prudence's voice advising her. "Snowdrift-proof and warm. And cheap."

Gerry wished Prudence was here now, then chided herself. "She's on a beach in St. Lucia. Well, no, she isn't. She's asleep in her hotel room. But soon she'll be on a beach. Though knowing her, she's probably up and trying to organize the hotel restaurant. Or cleaning her room herself. Sorry, cats." She addressed the two—Bob and Jay—who'd followed her to the back door, thinking breakfast was an hour-and-a-half early. "I'll be back soon. I hope."

She slammed the door and quickly walked to Blaise Parminter's house next door.

He was her only near neighbour on this side of the main road of Lovering. To the northwest of Gerry's was a large abandoned house. Of course her cousin Andrew lived across the street and her dear friend Cathy Stribling occupied her bed and breakfast Fieldcrest next door to Andrew. But Blaise Parminter was very old—in his nineties—and Gerry felt especially responsible for him, as well as his cat, formerly one of Gerry's Aunt Maggie's, but given by Gerry to Blaise to assuage the old man's loneliness.

Anyway, the cat (Graymalkin, Blaise called him, after the devilish familiar to one of *Macbeth*'s witches) preferred the man and his solitary lifestyle; had been continually fighting with the other cats when he'd lived at The Maples. His name there had been Stupid and Gerry still had to make an effort not to call him that.

She walked at the side of the road and knocked on Blaise's front door. She noticed the Christmas wreath hanging there was looking a bit the worse for wear and made a mental note to check her own. Or take it down. Apparently, January weather wasn't doing Blaise's wreath any good.

He must have been waiting for her, as the door opened almost immediately. "Come in! Come in! Thank you for coming. He's not anywhere. I've been calling and calling. I'm afraid he's stuck in a room upstairs and I'm not really supposed to climb stairs anymore."

Gerry had been divesting herself of her outerwear, saw her friend's anxious face, and held up a hand. "Blaise, make us a pot of tea and sit down while I have a good look around." He shuffled towards the kitchen and Gerry bounded up the first flight of stairs.

New territory to her, as there had never before been a reason for her to go upstairs in Blaise's multi-storey Victorian "monstrosity," as she affectionately called it. As Gerry had expected, there were many nooks and crannies, which increased in number when she went up the narrower second flight of stairs to what she supposed would have once been servants' rooms or nurseries.

"Stu—Graymalkin," she called, as she prowled from one room to another. A bed in one, an unused-looking desk in another, boxes in a third. She opened various cupboards and checked the windows in case the cat had found a way out.

In the room with a bed she dragged a chair over to a high wardrobe, stepped up and ran her hands along its top. She dusted off her hands, then looked more closely at them. Chalk? She reached up again. Yes. Chalk. Or something like it.

She hopped off the chair and onto the bed, further away from the wardrobe. This allowed her to see the hole. It was in the corner where the wall met the ceiling. "Awfully small for a cat to go through," she muttered doubtfully.

She went out of the room and prowled the hall, looking up. Ah. A square door in the ceiling. She bustled downstairs to the kitchen.

"The good news, Blaise, is I've found a hole leading to the attic in the ceiling of one of the top-floor bedrooms. Squirrels must have chewed through the drywall. The bad news is I don't hear anything up there." She grasped the mug of tea he offered her and swigged half of it. "How do I get into the attic?"

"I haven't been up there in years. Let me think. You push up the ceiling door with a pole. The door's on hinges. Then I just used to use a stepladder." He wrung his hands. "Oh, I hope you find him, Gerry."

"I will," she assured him. She looked at the kitchen clock. Seven o'clock. Lots of time until she'd have to leave for her one o'clock class. She chugged the rest of her tea and, grasping a mop, a flashlight and a stepladder, slowly made her way back to the third floor, trying not to gouge any wallpaper. Blaise sat on the steps in the hall, waiting.

Gerry stood halfway up the ladder and tentatively pushed with the sponge-end of the mop. The door barely shifted. "Right," she said determinedly, and gave a sudden hard shove. The square rose, hovered, then disappeared and banged down on the attic floor. "Success!" she shouted and heard a mumble from Blaise far away. She ascended the ladder and poked her head up into the dark.

Blaise had not used the attic for storage (except for a pile of lumber), which was a good thing, as every surface was coated in dust and much of the airspace was taken up by fantastic cobwebs, some collapsed and ancient, others all too active looking. Gerry grimaced. "Ugh. Reminds me of Cathy's basement."

She climbed up into the attic and, using the flashlight like a machete through underbrush, thrust aside webs as she checked out the perimeter of the room.

No cat that she could see. It was too dark low down in the corners to see a hole from the bedroom below. A way out? She went to inspect the tiny window at the front of the house. No exit here. She walked to the rear of the house. Not a window exactly, but a slatted vent, out which one could see the lake. Just barely. One of the slats, low down, was missing.

Gingerly, Gerry poked the flashlight through, and was rewarded by seeing its light shine on a little ledge stained by bird droppings. "So he could get out," she murmured. "The little monkey." She hastily ran back downstairs to tell Blaise.

"He's not up there but he could get out and then grapple his way down the tree, the one with the reddish bark."

"The wild cherry," Blaise said, and led the way to the kitchen. Gerry slid the back door open and they both stepped out. Blaise stayed close to the house while Gerry located the tree and looked in the snow near its base.

"I think I see some tracks, but they're leading in various directions. When the sun comes up, they'll be easier to read." She looked at Blaise's face, pinched with worry. "Blaise, do you have medication you're supposed to take when you wake up?"

"Well, I…yes, I do…but—"

"Go in and take it and don't worry. Shall I see if Cathy is free to help out?"

"Yes, all right. Here. Phone her."

Gerry checked the clock. 7:20. Cathy should be up. She was. "I can do the searching, Cathy, but Blaise needs some company." Cathy said she'd be right over. "Right. I'm going out now." She let herself out the back.

A weak light was appearing downriver, turning the snow from grey to soft creamy white. As Gerry had noticed before on other winter mornings, the sun would make the briefest of appearances before clouds blocked its glow for the rest of the day. It was as if it wished to give hope that somewhere, if not here, it was shining, that there was warmth.

She put the flashlight in her pocket and walked carefully, looking down. The most clearly used path led to her property. "Where would I go if I was Stupid?" She grinned. "That came out wrong. Okay, Graymalkin, I'm coming to find you."

She followed a confusion of tracks leading to the gate that separated Blaise's and her properties. She opened the gate and walked onto her land: the house yellow with white trim to her left; the ghostly remnants of last year's garden poking up through snow straight ahead. As she walked up the path to the house, she thought: I should get out here and shovel again. She looked for more tracks.

There was the distinctive hop and splotch left by a squirrel bounding from the base of one tree to another; there, under the apple tree, the longer marks of several rabbits; even the little long trails she jokingly assigned to "snow snakes," but which were made by small rodents—mice or voles—dragging their tiny forms through loose surface snow.

She kept along the back of the house and up onto the narrow decked walkway. So if Gray—I'll just call him Gray in my mind, far easier—so if he came this way, when he got to here (here was the side parking area between her kitchen door and shed), he would go...where?

Anywhere, her logical brain told her. To the road even. Oh, no! She quickly checked both sides of the road from her house to Blaise's and back. At that moment her cousin Andrew came out of his pleasant two-storey cottage—white with black trim and roof, red shutters.

He peered down at her from his great height. "Gerry. What's up? You jogging now?"

"Hardly, Andrew. I mean, in January?"

"Some do."

"No, well, I'm looking for Blaise's cat. He seems to have gotten out in the night and not come home."

Andrew thought. "It wasn't too cold last night. About zero. Nothing a healthy cat couldn't survive. If he found a warm place."

Gerry mused. "A warm place." They both turned to look at the abandoned house next to hers. "Do you think...?"

He shrugged. "Maybe. Must be lots of ways for animals to get in. Look at the cracked glass in that window up there. If you can get in without breaking anything, go for it. It's obvious the owners don't care about the place."

She paused. "When are you leaving, Andrew?" She referred to his proposed visit to Cathy's sister Markie who lived in Arizona and whom they'd all met over Christmas. The attraction between Andrew and Markie had been immediate and obvious.

Andrew blushed and smiled, his homely face made attractive. "About a week, ten days. Depends on Markie's work."

She smiled. "Well, soak up some sun for me."

"Will do. Gotta dash." He got into his car and drove away.

I hope that works out for them, she thought. Gosh, it must be about eight by now. She went home, made a coffee and fed the cats. Then she phoned Blaise. “Hello?” he quavered.

“Hi, Blaise. I’m just feeding my mob and then I’m going back out to look some more. Is Cathy there?”

There was a bump and a rustle and then Gerry heard Cathy’s clear tones. “Gerry?”

“I checked the road, Cath. No body. So that’s good. I’m going down to the lake next—”

Cathy interrupted her. “You won’t go on the ice, Gerry? It’s too soft.”

“No, I won’t. But it would hold a cat. I’m looking for tracks. Then I’ll try the house next door. He might have crawled in there. So I’ll be another hour or so. Keep Blaise calm.”

“Will do.”

Gerry put her coffee in a travel mug and went outside. Bob, who, of all her cats, seemed to mind winter the least, followed her. They stared at the lake. The hole where two of her acquaintances had gone through and one had drowned a few weeks before had refrozen, but she thought she could pinpoint the spot. What if the cat had gone out there in the early hours of the morning? And fallen through? They’d never know what had happened to him. She walked down to the shore.

A glint of red in a small tree made her look up. She reached and pulled the bough toward her. “Look, Bob, Christmas ribbon.” She unwound it from the branch and put it in her pocket. Christmas really is over, she thought glumly.

Bob ventured out onto the edge of the ice, sniffing. Gerry went a little ways out but a cracking sound made her retreat. She compared Bob’s tracks with some others, similar but much larger. A dog? Dogs? She remembered the howl she thought she’d heard last night and pictured wolves or coyotes running across the frozen river on the hunt. Hunting a cat, out at night prowling? She shivered, imagining how they'd tear their prey apart. "But there would be blood. And fur. Wouldn't there, Bob?"

Bob was oblivious, bounding through the deep snow that led from Gerry's yard through the thicket and so to the empty house next door. He stopped and looked over his shoulder as if to say, "Hey, Bigfoot, come and make a path," which Gerry did, stepping over him and shuffling with her feet together. He followed close behind, making little clicking noises.

"What? Do you smell your old buddy, Stupid? I mean Gray. And he's more of an enemy, isn't he?" When they reached the thicket, it was every man for himself, as Gerry pushed against old burdocks, bramble bushes and thorny shrubs and Bob twisted between stalks and trunks, sinking into snow with a pained look on his face.

She thought she heard a cat mew and looked up. She did a double take. Had Jay escaped? No. This was a much larger cat, though identical in markings to Jay—black with white legs—lurking around the back of the house. "I wonder," she murmured, but stumbling, looked down, and when she again looked up, the cat had made itself scarce.

Finally they were through. Gerry looked around. She'd never been on this property before. It looked larger than her own, with fewer trees, at least at this end of the lot. The land sloped gently up from where she was standing toward a small wood past the house. She had a dim memory of the house being quietly occupied when she was a child visiting Aunt Maggie, but not of any person in particular.

It was in pretty bad shape. Windows were boarded up. Some strips of siding were missing. Bits of the eaves sagged and one downspout had come away completely, rested at an angle in a snowdrift. The roof tiles were curled and flaking.

Yet once it must have been a lovely house, painted white with black window frames, long and low with lots of views of the lake. Some of the delicate lacy trim still remained, delineating the roofline. A few windowpanes, high up, retained a distinctive diamond-paned pattern. "Miss Havisham," Gerry muttered, "waiting in her mouldy wedding dress," and shuddered at the image. "That would make a creepy drawing."

Bob, meanwhile, neither impressed by architecture nor distracted by literary allusions, was nosing around in the backyard. He sniffed, stiffened and retreated up a tree, only to smell along one long thick bough and hastily rejoin Gerry on the ground. "Whoa, Bob, found something scary?" She examined the tracks under the tree and followed them to the back door.

They were different from any Gerry had previously seen, bigger than a cat's, oval where most cats' or dogs' were round. She sucked in her breath when she saw the long claw marks in the snow. There were cat tracks as well, and her worry for Blaise's cat increased. "Yikes, no wonder you're freaked out. Come here." She picked Bob up in her arms. "You don't want to meet up with the owner of those."

Bob struggled to be let go and disappeared around the far side of the house. Before she followed him, Gerry bent over and looked closely at a hole in the siding low to the ground. Big enough for a cat, she reasoned, or perhaps whatever possessed those frightening claws. She went to look for Bob and found him sitting in a window box with one paw hooked under the edge of a board that had been hammered on to cover a window. Gerry looked furtively toward the road. No one passing. She pulled on the board and it came away easily, its wood crumbling in the nail holes. "Rotten," she said and set it down under the window, which, to her surprise, was intact. So the plywood was to protect the glass not instead of it, she realized. She pushed the window up. As it opened, Bob darted in. "In for a penny," she muttered, pushing it all the way up, stepping in and closing it behind her.

She looked around and took out her flashlight. Mostly empty of furniture, the house was as dusty and dirty as Blaise's attic.

Dirtier, as mouse poop littered the floor. But she could see that it might be habitable. By the time she thought to look for cat tracks, Bob had trotted around the first room and the second before disappearing.

Gerry shone the light up the stairs. A single set of cat footprints had disturbed the dust. "Bob?" He appeared from behind her and bounded up the stairs. She followed, whispering, "Were those your tracks?"

Bob and Gerry prowled from room to room. Her reflection in a mirror in one room startled her, as did the glimpse of a dressmaker's dummy in another. She heard Bob's low growl start and abruptly stop. "Bob?" She shone her light into another room. There he was, crouched, tail thrashing, his hairs puffed. A string of old-fashioned Christmas lights with large bulbs lay on the floor.

Gerry could see nothing to make him behave so. She picked him up. "Well, you must have made those tracks coming up the stairs. Gray's not here. Let's go home."

Once out the window, she propped its plywood cover partially over the glass and walked around to the front of the house. More boarded-up windows. The path from the gate in the white picket fence looked like it might have been shovelled that winter but fresh drifts of snow made it hard to tell. There were partially obscured human footprints leading to the front door, and on its peeling surface someone had hung a faded Christmas wreath.

# 3

Gerry let herself and Bob into her house and checked the time. 9:20. She called Blaise. Cathy picked up. "Anything?"

"I don't think so but I found some wicked tracks in the snow. Long curved nails."

"A fisher," Cathy crisply said, then lowered her voice. "They kill cats. I hope Graymalkin is hiding. What now?"

"I'm going to shower and change. I teach my first art history class today so I have to leave at 12:30. Twelve-fifteen would be better because of finding parking. But tell Blaise I'll be over in a few minutes."

Gerry whisked in and out of the shower, dithered a bit over what to wear to school, settled on a white turtleneck with a pink sweater and blue jeans. No need to *really* dress up. After all, it was art history, not law. She quickly cleaned the cats' six litter boxes, lined up in the downstairs toilet, topped up the kibble tub and adjusted the thermostat. "Don't want you guys to be cold," she said as she passed through the dining room. "I'll make a nice cozy fire tonight."

Sleepy eyes blinked at her as the cats sitting on chairs around the large dining room table digested her words. The black and white kitten, Jay, a tuxedo cat like Bob, rolled on the ancient oriental carpet, Mother giving her fond supervision.

Gerry petted the kitten. "I'm sorry, sweetie, I don't have time to play. Wait." She retrieved her coat and fished in one pocket. "Here." She dangled the red ribbon in front of Jay who snagged it with one claw and rolled under the table in a ball of ribbon-shredding fun.

Gerry straightened up. "Make sure she doesn't swallow any, Mother." The marmalade tiger looked at Gerry indignantly. "All right, I know you will," Gerry soothed. "Bye, guys."

She threw her course notes into her car, then trudged back to Blaise's. Testing the front door, she found it open and let herself in.

Blaise and Cathy sat in the kitchen drinking tea and eating toast. Gerry helped herself to a piece of toast, slathering it with butter and marmalade. "I'm famished!"

Cathy, a middle-aged lady whose comfortable shape revealed her fondness for cooking and eating, poured her a cup of tea. Gerry swallowed a mouthful. "I checked the empty house next door to mine but I don't think Graymalkin was ever in there. I had to pry off one of the window covers. It's in not too bad shape inside."

"Only been empty twenty years or so," Cathy supplied.

Blaise put down his cup and asked, "What do you think happened to Graymalkin, Gerry?"

She swallowed again and replied nervously, "Well, there are tracks out there of other animals but no evidence that anything was wounded or…or eaten." Blaise sucked in a breath in consternation. Cathy patted one of his hands.

Gerry stood up. "I better close the attic door and put away your ladder, Blaise. Then we'll decide what next to do."

As she left the room, she heard Blaise say, "People put up posters, don't they? When they lose a pet? And I'll offer a reward." Cathy's reply was indistinguishable, her tones comforting as Gerry mounted the first flight of stairs. She felt a lump in her throat as she realized how anguished Blaise must be feeling.

It was when she was halfway up the second flight that she thought she heard something. She ran to the ladder positioned beneath the attic trap door. Yes! She'd heard a mew! Forgetting political correctness, she called, "Stupid! Stupid! Where are you?" and climbed the ladder.

As her eyes adjusted to the dim light, she heard another mew. It reminded her of the little mews kittens make. She looked around wildly. The pile of lumber? She looked all around it, pushing aside a piece of wood with her toe. Something lay there, very still. She stood over it. "Oh, my God!"

It was Stupid. But what had done this to him? Gerry put out a tentative hand. She and Stupid had history from when he'd been just another one of the cats inherited from Aunt Maggie. He'd been defiantly unaffectionate, had scratched her several times before she'd given up on him. It had been a relief when Blaise took him off her hands.

"Stupid," she said softly and knelt in the dust. "Graymalkin, I know we don't like each other, but your Blaise can't come up here to get you and you need help." She laid a hand softly on his head. Again he made the pathetic little mew. Encouraged, Gerry slid her left hand under his shoulders and her right under his hips before slowly dragging him towards her.

She felt sick. His blood had soaked the floor where he'd lain. In one motion, trying to keep her hands as steady as possible, she lifted him to her chest and stood. "Okay. Okay now." She backed toward the opening in the floor and knelt; slid her left arm to completely support him and felt for the opening with her right hand. "Okay, Gray. I'm almost organized here." She folded him to her chest and felt him go limp. Slowly, she kicked out with her right foot until she found the plastic top of the stepladder, remembering the warning printed on it: THIS IS NOT A STEP. "Well, today it is," she mumbled, "and I don't weigh very much."

With relief, she reached the first real step with her left foot and continued down, encouraging the cat softly as she went. Once off the ladder, she looked at his face. His eyes were closed and he was panting, his tongue hanging out of his mouth. Shock, she thought. Down on the second level she found the bathroom, spread a big towel on the floor and wrapped the cat in it. She went down to the entranceway and thought quickly. "Cathy," she called quietly. Cathy came into the hall, her face changing from curiosity to concern. "Can you drive us to the vet? He's very bad."

"Yes, yes, but—" she jerked her head toward the kitchen.

"Tell him it's an emergency and we have to move fast."

But Blaise had appeared in the kitchen door. "Oh, you found him, Gerry! Thank you! Thank you!"

"He's very ill, Blaise. Cathy and I are going to speed to the vet. We'll call you from there. I'm going now." She didn't want him to see all the blood, and fumbled the front door open. "Meet you at my car, Cathy." She called over her shoulder, "Grab my coat, would you?"

Cathy caught up to her halfway to The Maples. She draped Gerry's coat around her shoulders. Gerry said, with a catch in her throat, "He's almost cut in two, Cathy. I didn't want Blaise to see him like this."

Cathy, who loved her own pet dog intensely, stifled a groan and scurried ahead to open Gerry's car, then got behind the wheel. "Oh, cripes! Manual shift. All right. I drove my dad's sports car when I was young. Here goes." She backed the Mini out of the driveway and drove towards Lovering. "We'll go to Dr. Morin. She's closest and she's very good." Gerry, who hadn't yet needed a vet for any of her numerous felines, said nothing.

Gray was still breathing, but barely. "He's lost a lot of blood," she said quietly as they arrived at the vet's. Cathy opened Gerry's door and they quickly entered the vet's.

"Emergency," Gerry gasped. The receptionist took one look at the unconscious cat and blood-soaked towel and buzzed for the vet.

An elegant white-coated woman with nicely arranged hair and polished nails joined them. She had a technician dressed in dark blue scrubs with her. "Take him through, Sophie," she told her assistant. "If he lives long enough, he'll need a transfusion," she said to Gerry. "Expensive."

Gerry gulped. "Yes, yes, anything. But I'm not the owner." The vet disappeared after Gray and the technician. The receptionist took over. "Would you like to call the owner?" she asked sympathetically. "Ask their permission? There might be an operation." She handed Gerry a portable phone. Gerry, beginning to shake, handed it to Cathy and pulled her jacket around her more closely.

She became aware of Cathy speaking to Blaise on the phone and of the other clients in the waiting room watching and listening. The receptionist made a short announcement. "I'm so sorry. Dr. Morin is now in surgery. I've called Dr. Perry and he should be here shortly to look after your pets. Or, if someone can't wait, I will reschedule their appointment." There was a bit of murmuring, but the owners of the more or less healthy dogs and cats were probably so thankful it wasn't their cat going for surgery, they settled down.

"I can't believe I missed him the first time I checked. If he hadn't mewed..."

"But you did find him. He must have been unconscious the first time. And it was probably dark up there."

Gerry nodded. "He crawled under the planks to die, I suppose. Reminds me of when...what time is it?"

Cathy consulted her wristwatch. "A quarter to eleven. Reminds you of when Marigold died?"

Gerry relaxed and nodded. The cat in question, Aunt Maggie's favourite, had recently died of old age and had crawled into a cupboard before Gerry found her. "Okay. I can wait here until noon, drive you home and still make my art class."

"Why do that? It's going to be a while. Blaise is terribly upset. Drive me home now. I'll make him some lunch and you can arrive with lots of time to spare."

Gerry stood up. "All right." They told the receptionist what was happening, Gerry went to wash the blood off her hands and they left. Gerry dropped Cathy at Blaise's and continued to a fast-food restaurant drive-through. "Comfort me," she muttered, as she ordered a burger and large fries. She drove to the college and ate in the car.

As she rushed to the Fine Arts building, a large luxury car driven by a sour-faced man almost cut her off at a crosswalk. One passenger stared at her without blinking—the boy from yesterday's tour. Two girls sat in the back seat.

She gave the boy a polite smile and the driver a steely-eyed glare as she walked in front of the car. She stuffed her fast-food garbage hurriedly into a bin outside the entrance. The boy got out of the car and brushed past her. She managed a brief hello, which went unacknowledged, then caught sight of the driver glaring at her before he drove away. She shrugged and went to her class.

The room was already full. As she took off her coat and turned to face the students, she heard a collective gasp followed by some snickering and much murmuring. They were all looking at her chest. She looked down. She was covered in blood.

Back in her car after the class, she would have laughed if she hadn't been so worried about the cat.

She'd briefly explained how the blood got on her sweater. She'd peeled off the sweater only to find blood had soaked through onto her white turtleneck. She'd made the best of it, turning off the lights for a visual overview of the course made by the instructor she was replacing.

"How," she'd asked, "did we get from this"—she'd clicked on the image of a romantic Renoir—"to this?" and clicked again to a Picasso nude. She'd told them how the course would unfold over the semester as they discussed historical context and the development of painting techniques, and what she would expect from them. There were groans when she delineated the required reading and number of papers and presentations. And when she wrapped it up ten minutes early, there were sighs of relief.

She leaned back in the car. All in all, not too bad. As she turned the key, she wondered if her clothes were salvageable.

On the drive home, she let her mind relax. She took the river road instead of the highway whenever she wasn't in a rush, and enjoyed its gorgeous views of the Lake of Two Mountains, part of the Ottawa River, as well as the both modest and fabulous homes along the way.

Huts meant to shelter ice fishermen dotted the frozen surface of the lake but no one was out there today. The thaw had made the ice too dangerous. A chain across the access road barred cars from entering.

The view changed as the road left the shore to meander between riverside properties and farmlands. She passed the ferry entrance. Another chain indicated that the operators had closed the ice road. When it freezes hard again, I should drive over, she thought. I seem to remember there's a good french-fry stand on the other side.

She passed Blaise's house and pulled into her own driveway with relief. A long day, not yet over. Cats, she remembered, and entered her house.

Cathy called with an update. "And the vet said it might be days before she brings him back to consciousness—if he makes it. She can't operate to close the wound until she's sure it's not infected—as it was probably a wild animal attack. The poor cat is sedated; he's got a drain or something in the wound. Oh, and the wound's not all the way around like you thought, but on one side, from spine to belly."

Gerry took a deep breath. "At least he's still alive. I'm relieved. How's Blaise?"

Cathy's voice changed tone and she spoke cautiously. "He seems all right but I know he's very upset. I'm taking him to see the cat tomorrow."

"Oh, that's good of you."

"Well, I imagine how I'd feel if it were Charles who was hurt." Charles was Prince Charles, Cathy's beloved basset cross. Crossed with something with wavy hair, he was a delightful dog—if you liked them overweight and sleepy. Which Cathy obviously did, as Charles was her treasure.

"How is Charles?" Gerry asked, humouring her friend.

"He's fine. He'd like to wear that fine red coat you got him for Christmas but it's been too mild. Strange weather, eh?" She didn't wait for Gerry to reply. "How was your first class?"

"Oh, all right. They paid pretty good attention, considering I looked like I'd just murdered someone."

"What? Oh, no! Cat blood on your clothes. I never noticed because you put your coat on at the vet and then—oh dear. Did you clean them yet? Soak them in cold water overnight, Gerry, then scrub them tomorrow."

"Mm." Gerry thought of the sweater and top, already in the garbage. "Cathy, I've got to go. I'm exhausted. And my cats need some attention."

"Of course they do. I'll keep you informed about Graymalkin." She rang off.

Gerry trudged upstairs and ran a bath. She added some fragrant salts she'd received from Cathy at Christmas and luxuriated in the silky water. A scratch at the door disturbed her relaxation. She groaned and heaved herself out of the bath, opened the door. Bob and the miniature version of him, Jay the kitten, sat there. "Oh, come in, if you're going to. All the lovely steam is leaving the room."

She resettled in the hot water. Bob easily jumped onto the edge of the tub. Scrabbling sounds told her Jay was unable. She reached over the side and picked the kitten up. It stood uncertainly on the tub's slick surface. Gerry wrung out her washcloth and set the kitten on it. Bob had already made himself comfortable, lying along the length of the porcelain.

"Sorry, Bob, no bubbles to play with." He blinked. The kitten's bright eyes took it all in. Gerry dozed.

Splash! Gerry opened her eyes as Jay clawed at her leg. She clasped the kitten and reached for a towel. As she rose, wrapped the soaking cat and stepped out of the bath, she burst into tears. "Poor Stupid," she crooned, holding Jay. "Poor cat."

After that she felt better, went downstairs and made her supper: mac'n'cheese from a box with salad from a bag to make her feel virtuous. She looked at the various piles of work on the table as she ate. Damn it! She'd already worked today. She went to one of the bookcases, looked through her aunt's collection and pulled out *The Pictorial Encyclopedia of the Animal Kingdom* by V. J. Stanek.

It thunked down on the table. Heavy. She scraped the rest of the macaroni out of the pot and onto her plate. She was ashamed to admit she could eat the entire box in one meal. Her mother had used to serve the treat with hot dogs but Gerry didn't have any. Anyway, that would have meant dirtying another pot. As a cook, she liked to think of herself as a minimalist. She added a bit more salad to make up for the carbs and opened the book at its index.

Nothing under "fisher." She flipped through the book. Photography had certainly improved in the forty or so years since it had been published. It was a textbook, really, or the material had been presented in textbook style.

Almost all the pictures were in black and white. The author had begun with simple creatures—all the *-zoa* Gerry remembered from high school biology: corals, sea creatures, insects (Gerry flinched at the spiders) and fish. From there through reptiles and birds before arriving at the furry creatures—some cute, some not so cute. When she got to the weasel family, she stopped. Wolverine.

"Listen to this, cats. 'Though it is said it prefers fawns, it is said that it can kill fully grown elks or reindeer by leaping on their backs and biting them in the jugular veins.'" She raised her head from the book. "Holy cow. I don't think a cat would have any chance against one of those." Judging by the cats' demeanours, their self-confidence seemed undiminished. She turned the page.

Several relatives of the wolverine seemed too small to take on a cat. She passed over skunks and badgers before stopping at a photo of a small creature with a wicked expression, the pine marten. "'During the day it sleeps in hollow trees, at night it hunts small vertebrates, being even more at home in the trees than the squirrel, which is one of its favourite victims.' Huh. If it can catch a squirrel, it could certainly catch a cat. Maybe a marten is like a fisher. Oh, well." She closed and put away the book. "Something hurt Gray and if it could hurt him, it could hurt you guys. I'll have to think about this before I let you out in the spring. Or just keep you inside at night?"

She made a fire. More cats joined those already in the living room. It was interesting to see how the cats formed little social groups within the greater tribe. Harley and Kitty-Cat, her two enormous white and black "cow" cats, sat side by side, their paws tucked underneath their substantial chests.

The honour guard, made up of the cats that used to share Aunt Maggie's bed and still slept there—Blackie, Whitey, Mouse and Runt—were a female pride. They clustered to one side of the hearth.

Mother and Jay sat close together, while Bob, the three grey tigers called Winnie, Frank and Joe, and Ronald, a little cat—white except for a thin black moustache—formed a male pride and occupied the central position in front of the fire.

The other five—Min-Min, Cocoon, Max, Jinx and Monkey—were a loose association, sometimes mingling with other groups and tonight were dotted around the room. Only Lightning, an individual whose past severe physical trauma had warped her personality—she had suffered burns, it was thought, and was missing most of her tail as well as the fur of her hind legs—kept to herself. Gerry made a special effort with her, and the cat did sleep on her bed. But she didn't enjoy being petted—much—and seemed to avoid intimacy. She crouched under the table.

Gerry spoke aloud. "You know, in a way, this is ridiculous!" Nineteen little faces either turned to her or remained impassive. "I mean—look at us. A woman sitting by a fire with nineteen cats. Who does that?"

There were no comments from the felines, just a hissing from the fire when a bit of oozing maple sap collected on the end of a log, then dropped into hot coals. Through the ancient walls of The Maples, a wind could be heard rising then falling, rising then falling. The temperature outside began to drop.

# 4

Gerry had slept in. Well, if you call 8:30 sleeping in. Cat stomachs began rumbling around eight, but they were usually patient enough to give her that extra half hour.

Bob flicked a paw amongst the long red tangles that lay on the pale green pillowcase. He was behind her head in the space between her pillow and the wall. She tensed, then rolled, grabbing him. He pretended to struggle, then relaxed. Lightning, alert for any trouble even in her sleep, had zoomed off the matching quilted pale green bedcover and out of the room as soon as Gerry had made her move.

She pulled on robe and slippers and went downstairs. "It's sunny!" she said delightedly, seeing how the light was pouring into the back of the house. "How lovely!" A blue jay screeched and landed on a windowsill. A cardinal fluttered up into a bare shrub. In the kitchen she checked the thermometer mounted outside one window. "Brr. We're back in winter, cats." She went through the morning routine of feeding, cleaning litter boxes and making a fire, then took her coffee to her workstation at the living room table, still in her robe.

First, she gave *Mug the Bug* some attention. After all, he was her biggest earner. Then she reviewed the content for the next day's art history lesson. "Time to get particular and detailed," she muttered. The cats, familiar with this behaviour, their stomachs full, ignored her and dispersed. Some stayed by the warming hearth while others were more comfortable sleeping elsewhere.

Min-Min, a big white shorthair with green eyes, stood on his hind legs and patted Gerry's thigh. Deaf, he rarely mewed. He was elderly and a bit overweight, probably arthritic, so she picked him up and put him in her lap. With one hand she caressed his fur. He began a faint purr. With the other hand she made notes.

The course would rely heavily on French artists of the latter half of the nineteenth century. France had been the cultural centre of Europe at that time. Artists came from all over the world to study there. That was one of the ways Asian art influenced the Impressionists. And then some artists travelled to Asia themselves and were influenced there.

Gerry sighed. It was going to be a complicated and pleasurable task to collate all the material and present it. She'd pulled out her own art history notes and text books, not so out of date, as she'd graduated less than five years ago.

That reminded her: her twenty-sixth birthday was coming up—February 19—in about a month. What a change-filled year twenty-five had been! She'd moved from Toronto, the biggest city in Canada, to a village, population 5,000, in the province of Quebec; went from renting an apartment to owning a large house; and from zero pets to almost twenty!

She pulled a book towards her. An overview of art history, it would serve as her guide. She began.

Her growling stomach reminded her to eat. The morning had passed. She stretched. Sunlight made the backyard snow glisten. She dressed and thought about going for a walk. The phone rang. It was Cathy.

"I'm next door, Gerry, with Blaise. We visited Graymalkin. He's still unconscious but stable."

"That's good news, isn't it? How's Blaise?"

"Tired but hopeful. Gerry, the vet said you mustn't let your cats outside at dawn or dusk and definitely not at night. Whatever wild animal did this might be living in the area."

"What the—?" Gerry broke off and stared out at her backyard.

"Gerry? Gerry?" She heard Cathy's voice from a distance.

"Gotta go, Cathy. Tell you later." Gerry put on her boots and grabbed her jacket. She also grabbed a broom and rushed outside.

Bounding across her yard was what looked like a wolf.

Gerry stood in the parking pad at the side of the house, within reach of the door if she had to make a quick retreat. The wolf trotted from tree to tree, sniffing. It ran down to the shore, lifted one front paw and looked uncertainly at the ice. Turning, it caught sight of Gerry and headed towards her, mouth open, looking hungry.

A blond wolf? Gerry thought. She pointed the broom at the beast. "Back!" she ordered it. It sat in the snow and scratched one ear with a hind paw. Its tongue lolled. It rolled in the snow, making a vulpine snow angel.

"Oh, for heaven's sake!" Gerry leaned the broom next to the kitchen door. The wolf jumped up and shook, its tail wagging hopefully, its enormous ears almost fully retracted. It smiled and wiggled closer; then, bum in the air, the front portion of its body bowed. Gerry went inside the tiny kitchen porch and retrieved a handful of cat kibble from the large sack kept there. She flung a morsel at the beast and it snapped it out of the air. By now it was only a few feet away. Gerry threw again. It missed and snuffled on the icy asphalt. Then it sat and offered a paw. Gerry gravely shook hands and fed it again. "Now what?" she wondered aloud.

"Harriet!" was heard from afar. The cry was repeated. "Harriet! Harriet!" A young man, dressed in black ski pants and a red ski jacket, ran by the driveway, saw Gerry and doubled back. "Harriet! Have you been mooching?" The dog cringed and wagged her way over to him.

"Is she yours?" Gerry asked. The dog jumped, her paws on his chest. He nodded. White blond, the dog had the tightly curled tail of a husky but the large pricked ears of a German shepherd. Her back, the tip of her tail and the edges of her ears were all highlighted a delicate fox-red. Her nose was pink and black and her eyes a pale brown. Gerry added, "She's gorgeous. Is she a husky?"

Her owner was nice-looking too, she thought. Tallish, medium build; dark eyes and hair. Gerry realized she'd been staring and turned to look at the dog. The man was speaking. "A husky something cross. I thought she'd stick around if I was outside but evidently, no. I'll have to get a chain and stake her."

"Where do you live?"

He pointed along the road in the direction of the church. "I'm renting the little farmhouse behind St. Anne's. I'm a ski instructor and Lovering is handy for the ski hills around here." He mentioned a couple Gerry (not a skier) had been vaguely aware of.

She found she was tongue-tied and awkwardly patted the dog. "Harriet the husky," she said. The dog licked her hand and sniffed her pockets.

"Well, thank you for finding her," the man said uncertainly.

Gerry snapped out of her daze and introduced herself. "Gerry Coneybear. Artist. My house." She took a deep breath and laughed—too loudly, she thought. "I've got nineteen cats." Idiot, she called herself silently. You don't say that to someone you've just met.

He replied. "Thibeault. Jean-Louis. Pleased to meet you." He grinned. "Only one pet. So far. Come on, Harriet. See you, Gerry." He snapped a leash on Harriet. As they walked away, Gerry wondered if she should have told him about the attack on Graymalkin. Nah. A big dog like that would be fine.

After lunch she decided not to waste the sunny day by staying inside. "I can work tonight," she told Bob as she put on a sweater and light jacket. "Sorry, buddy." She edged out the kitchen door, using her foot to keep him from following her. She unlocked the shed and stepped inside.

"I've got to organize this place this spring," she murmured, stepping over sacks of birdseed and manure in the little front room used for plant-related activities. "And repair it."

In the main area of the shed, lots of tools and unwanted furniture were dumped on one side while her woodpile dominated the other. A blue tarp sagged from above where, on Christmas Eve, a tree had made a hole in the shed's roof, the same tree that had dented her car. It was darker than usual inside, as one of the windows, broken a few weeks earlier, was boarded up. That reminded her of the plywood she'd removed from the window of the house next door. She guiltily made a promise to fix it after her walk. She found her snowshoes and took them outside.

She shivered in the sub-zero weather, wearing only a thin jacket, but knew she'd soon be sweating. The snowshoes were the wide heavy old-fashioned ones made of wood and some kind of animal rawhide. She looked down at her feet. Kind of gross, really, the rawhide, but clever. She clumped down the road.

When she passed Andrew's house and the bit of field next to that, she turned right. This road doubled as a back driveway into Cathy's B&B and as the main driveway to a farmhouse far from the main road, perched on a slight rise among what Gerry had been told used to be cow pastures.

The driveway had been cleared as far as Cathy's property line, but after that there was snow for Gerry to play on. She swung her legs out and around and was soon trotting toward the farmhouse.

The family that owned it used it as a three-season cottage, so she didn't feel she was trespassing when she crossed the lawn in front of the empty house, swung left and headed into the trees. The path, made by snowmobilers (and bless their noisy hearts, Gerry thought, for compacting the trail), showed evidence cross-country skiers also were using it. She paused and listened.

Chickadees chirped and fluttered in pine trees. A hidden squirrel angrily warned Gerry to back off. She looked at what she at first thought was a squirrel's nest just above her head. But no squirrel would nest that close to the ground, would it?

On closer inspection, she realized the roundish tangle of twigs had been made by the tree, originating from a single area on one branch. She reached up and touched it. "Strange," she murmured. She continued through the woods across the train tracks and into the deeper woods.

There was the sugar shack where she'd gotten skunked last fall. She kept on past it and climbed the steeply sloping path that wound through giant maples. "Sweet trees," she said. She wondered if there would be sugaring off this spring. She remembered one perfect day from her early childhood.

It must have been the Easter weekend. After searching with her father for eggs hidden outside at The Maples where there was little snow left on the lawn, they'd gone inside where her mother and Aunt Maggie had been preparing blueberry pancakes with maple syrup. Then they'd all walked up to the sugar bush, Gerry being given rides on her father's shoulders when she tired.

Between the trees some snow remained. Uncle Geoff had been working collecting the sap, assisted by a skinny Andrew, barely out of his teens. Shortly, a young couple, each holding a small boy, had joined them. Gerry drew in her breath sharply at this memory. Her cousin Margaret and Doug, her then husband! With James and Geoff Jr. And David not yet born, she supposed.

She tried to remember any impression of the couple. Had they been happy at that time? What had Doug looked like? How had Margaret seemed? But her mind drew a blank. She supposed she'd been too busy flitting from tree to tree, lifting the lids of the maple sap buckets to inspect the levels inside and informing her male relatives when she'd found one brimming full of the clear liquid.

Of her Aunt Mary, she had no recollection. Perhaps the family's primitive fun in the sugar bush had been beneath her aunt. She remembered the steamy interior of the shack and the sweet odour of boiling sap. She remembered Uncle Geoff pouring some syrup onto clean snow and using maple twigs to make impromptu lollipops for the kids. And the adults. And that was all.

She left the sugar bush as she reached the top of the hill and entered the stand of pine planted by her late uncle. "Hello, Uncle Geoff," she said softly, and kept going.

The sky clouded over and it began to snow. Her way continued: now down, now up, but mostly straight. She could turn around and go home the way she'd come or she could make a left and continue; make a big circle for a really long walk. The fact that there was a restaurant on the highway where the path through the woods ended, and that they had hot chocolate gave her a third choice. She kept going towards the hot chocolate.

The path climbed again, followed alongside a small frozen creek that widened into a stream that deepened to run through a ravine. Water rushed beneath the stream's frozen surface, bubbling up here and there and making a pleasant sound. She paused and listened for a moment, absorbing the peace of the woodland scene in the falling snow. She heard a snowmobile's motor and prepared to step off the path. But it never got as far as where she was. She heard a second machine—its sound coming from a different direction—but it too never came near her.

She became aware of the sound of cars on the highway and suddenly she didn't want to leave the quiet of the woods. She turned around and retraced her steps.

She'd just reached the train tracks and had paused, catching her breath, when she heard another snowmobile coming fast, seemingly from behind her. She stepped over one rail so she stood between the tracks, backing away from the trail.

The roar of the snowmobile increased as it sped up the incline to where she waited. The driver paused, gave her a look, made a hard left and zoomed away alongside the tracks towards the centre of Lovering.

As he'd been wearing a dark blue suit and a black helmet with the tinted visor down, Gerry had no idea who it had been, except that he was large and probably male. It would have been nice if he'd at least waved. Or nodded. She shrugged and made her way home.

Light snow had covered her car and driveway, and the sun was setting, turning a white sky first silver and then a dark grey. It was cat supper and Gerry coffee time so she hurried inside.

After the beasts were satiated and a hazelnut vanilla latte was foaming in a bowl, she checked her phone answering machine. One message: Cathy, inviting her to supper. "No charge, dear," her friend, an excellent chef and caterer said. "I'm just lonely. Come as you are."

A sweaty Gerry decided coming as she was would be inappropriate and enjoyed a quick bath before changing into jeans and sweater. The sweater she would have preferred to wear was in the garbage so this one—an old red Christmas sweater, complete with Santa Claus driving his team and sleigh up and over a cute snow-covered cottage with Ho Ho Ho coming out of his mouth—would have to do. If I spill food on it, it certainly won't show, she thought. She rummaged for a bottle of wine and set off.

The snow had stopped. The cold crisp night enveloped her. She inhaled appreciatively. As someone who had spent most of her life in Toronto, she enjoyed the Quebec countryside—its fresh air, its space. She looked up at stars in a clear sky.

She walked up Cathy's main driveway. As usual, when entertaining, Cathy had her front rooms illuminated, and the big old house looked welcoming, like a lady spreading her skirts on a sofa, patting the space beside her and saying "Come and get comfy and we'll have a nice long chat." Gerry exhaled and rang the bell.

"Gerry!" Cathy kissed her and took her coat while Gerry kicked off her boots. "Thanks for coming. I really got used to having someone around when Markie was here and now the house feels—kind of empty."

Cathy's sister had visited after Christmas, helped distract Cathy from the fact that someone had been murdered in her basement. And Markie meeting Gerry's cousin Andrew and them hitting it off meant that Markie had delayed returning to her home in Arizona.

"I can see that," Gerry agreed. "I got used to having Prudence around." She didn't add that she'd also breathed a sigh of relief when Prudence had left for her vacation. An only child, Gerry was comfortable with solitude, needed it for her work.

Again as usual, Cathy seated her by the fire in the genteel, shabby living room and brought her a gin and tonic. Gerry smacked her lips. Charles, slumbering on the warm tiles of the hearth, had acknowledged her presence by opening one eye. She petted him, he sighed and closed it. "So?"

"So," Cathy replied, "the cat is still in a coma, but seems stable. Blaise is all right. I guess at his age, you've seen so much death, you become philosophical."

"And the expense?"

"It'll be a lot but, as Blaise says, he has no other dependants."

"Mm. I've figured out that this spring when my cats mostly all need their shots, I could be spending about three thousand at the vet's."

"Good grief!" Cathy seemed stunned. "Maybe you can work out a payment plan."

"If the auction of my Borduas is successful, I could clear a quarter of a million, maybe more. But it's already been delayed once. I don't know what they're waiting for."

"A quarter of a million! Good God!" This time Cathy really was stunned into silence. She brought a bowl of chips and one of dip from a sideboard. Charles struggled to roll from his side to his ample belly. He stared as Gerry transferred each chip from the large bowl to the smaller and from there into her mouth. She flung him a naked chip and he crawled toward it. Cathy looked fondly at this activity.

"Charles loves the snow. Today he—" But whatever the prince had done in or on the snow that day was fated to be known only to Charles and his owner, for at that moment, the doorbell rang. Cathy rose. "My other guest," she said, looking over her shoulder with an arch expression. Charles, refusing to be distracted from his mission, stayed fixated on Gerry.

Gerry sat up. She heard a male voice. Could Cathy have an admirer?

"Gerry, have you met Jean-Louis? You have?" Cathy seemed a bit disappointed.

Jean-Louis and Gerry nodded and smiled as Cathy mixed him a drink. "Over my dog," he said and raised his glass, sitting next to Gerry on the sofa. "*Santé*!"

"I just need to check something in the kitchen," Cathy murmured. Charles stayed with the guests, inching his way closer to the chip bowl.

"I didn't know anyone else was coming," said Gerry, self-consciously smoothing the Christmas sweater. This man certainly was handsome in his black turtleneck jersey and blue jeans. And his cologne was nice too.

"Me neither," he agreed, helping himself to a handful of chips. "My appetite increases as the temperature decreases."

"I know, right?" She helped herself likewise.

"Self-preservation. The body knows it should store fat."

By now Charles had crawled completely under the clear glass coffee table and his nose was positioned on the bit of carpet separating Gerry and Jean-Louis's feet. Unnerved by Jean-Louis's mention of the word "fat," and wondering if she should remove the bulky sweater, a large chip, well dipped in the delicious onion and sour cream concoction, dropped from Gerry's fingers. Trying to intercept it, Charles lurched upwards and banged his head sharply on the underneath of the table. He gobbled the chip before lapping dip off the carpet with a rather dazed look on his face.

Gerry and Jean-Louis looked at the dog. “Concussed?” Gerry asked.

“Definitely,” he replied. Charles had a hurt look on his face. They were giggling and snorting when Cathy returned.

“Well, you two seem to be getting along,” she commented smugly. And Gerry realized Cathy was matchmaking.

# 5

"Let's take this party into the kitchen! It's pizza night!" Cathy led the way to the back of the house.

As they passed the wide oak staircase, Jean-Louis said admiringly, "This is a lovely old building. If I weren't renting, I'd stay here."

"I've never had a boarder," Cathy rejoined. "Just short-term guests. Not that I'd mind," she added flirtatiously over her shoulder. She sat them at the kitchen table upon which a plethora of pizza toppings had been spread out.

"Mm," Gerry and Jean-Louis said simultaneously. Charles plodded determinedly into the room and plopped down between the table and the oven.

"Whoo, it's hot in here," Gerry said, gratefully peeling off the hideous sweater. Thankfully there was a clean white t-shirt underneath. They opened a bottle of wine and pointed to their preferred toppings.

Cathy expertly whapped pizza dough down on the counter and twirled it into shape. "Okay, Gerry, you're first." Gerry selected mozzarella, tomato sauce and basil. "Ah," said Cathy, "the classic Margherita," and popped the pizza into the oven. She assembled Jean-Louis's: pepperoni, ground beef, Swiss cheese and green peppers.

"Oh, throw some hot peppers on there too," he urged, smiling wickedly. "You only live once!"

"I'll drink to that!" Cathy toasted them. Jean-Louis refilled their glasses. Gerry's pizza was placed before her. She cut it in small segments and urged the others to sample.

Jean-Louis hesitated. "Does this mean I have to share mine with you when it's ready?"

"Ha!" Gerry riposted. "You're fooling nobody." The oven pinged and Jean-Louis's spicy meaty meal appeared. They cheered. He opened another bottle of wine. Cathy assembled her own pizza. Salmon, onions, capers and a crumbly mild cheese were topped with a drizzle of olive oil and fresh black pepper.

Jean-Louis exclaimed respectfully. "My God, Cathy, you know how to eat! Are you perhaps a Frenchwoman in disguise?"

Cathy sat down, her face flushed and happy. "No. The usual English mix—some Scottish, one grandmother from Wales. No French that I know of."

"I owe my fabulous English to my English mother."

And your dark good looks to your French father, Gerry dreamily reflected. Then she thought, I hope I didn't say that out loud. She licked her fingers.

By now, all their heads turned every time the timer pinged. "Pavlovian response," Gerry joked as Cathy's pizza made its appearance.

"Wait, wait! One more," the chef cried. "A group effort."

"Bacon!" Jean-Louis suggested.

"Cheddar!" was Gerry's contribution.

"Tomatoes!" Cathy said. "And olives."

They raised their glasses. "And olives!" they chimed. Jean-Louis opened the third bottle of wine as Cathy worked feverishly, popped pizza number four into the oven and collapsed to eat her own salmon extravaganza.

Prince Charles, having sampled everything, staggered to his water bowl and slurped noisily. The oven timer pinged and he swung his head. A quantity of water, hanging from his jowls, detached and slapped against a cupboard door.

"Oh, Charles! Gross! No, Cathy, you sit." Gerry released the last pizza from the oven and wiped dog slime from the cupboard. Charles, meanwhile, was back at his post—tableside.

Finally, they leaned back from the table. Compliments were paid to the chef, dishes loaded into the dishwasher and Cathy sent them to the living room while she prepared coffee.

Gerry collapsed onto the sofa. "I don't usually eat that much," she groaned.

Jean-Louis knelt by the fire and built it back up. The living room temperature provided a nice cool contrast to the heated kitchen, but the fire made the room cozy. He sat on the sofa and looked at her admiringly. "Your cheeks are all flushed."

Her hands rose to cover them. "Oh. They feel hot too. It's the wine, I guess, plus I went snowshoeing this afternoon. Must have caught some sun."

"I protect my skin against the weather," he replied primly.

"Oh yes?"

"You wouldn't believe the windburn one can get going down the side of a mountain."

Gerry recalled the ruddy faces of downhill skiers as she'd seen on television. "Yes, I guess it might be painful."

"I use a moisturizer and sunblock. I don't want to be all wrinkled by the time I'm forty."

"Um." Gerry really didn't have anything to add to this conversation. "Um. How old are you, Jean-Louis?"

"Call me J-L. That's what my mother does. I'm thirty-two."

"And you're a full-time ski instructor?"

"Yes. And in the summer I work as a trainer. It's fun. You, er, draw?"

"I'm a commercial artist, a cartoonist, really. And lately, I've become a teacher."

"Teaching art? Cathy, let me help you." He rose and took the tray from their hostess. Gerry's reply was lost in the bustle of adding cream and sugar to her coffee and enjoying the tiramisu Cathy had presented in shallow cut-glass bowls.

She beamed on the two younger ones. "Getting acquainted?"

"Yes. Yes, we are," J-L replied. "How many guests do you average a week, Cathy?"

As Cathy explained the seasonal vagaries of the hospitality trade, Gerry, to whom they were already familiar, let her mind drift.

After a moment she interrupted: "Do either of you know anything about trees making a kind of little shrub like a ball on one of their boughs? I thought they were squirrels' nests but one was low enough to examine and it was growing out of the tree."

J-L looked blank. Cathy mused for a second. "I think what you're describing might be a witch's broom. Wonderful name, eh?"

"Yeah. Creepy. Thanks." Gerry relapsed into a dream of women cutting sticks off trees, releasing the brooms and flying away into the night. She yawned.

"Somebody's sleepy," J-L teased.

Gerry stood. "Yes, I am. Cathy, thanks so much." She turned to J-L, half expecting him to offer to walk her home. He poured himself another cup of coffee then jumped up and kissed her on both cheeks.

"Lovely to meet you, Gerry. Again. Perhaps we'll meet in the woods sometime. I cross-country ski in there."

"Watch out for snowmobilers," she warned. "Today I heard several and had one come right up to me."

"Oh yes. Whereabouts?"

"Way up near the highway and again crossing the tracks."

Cathy accompanied Gerry to the front door and squeezed her arm. "Isn't he handsome?" she exclaimed but in a low voice.

"I think he's fun," Gerry admitted. "Thanks for the great food. I'll take you to lunch soon, okay? To pay you back. Cheer up, Charles," she said to the dog, which, with a sad expression, had wandered into the hall, and stooped to kiss his head.

Once again, she stepped out into the crisp clear night. The evening had been fun, hilarious even, but as the buzz from the wine ebbed and was replaced by a headache, Gerry felt that, somehow, it had all been a little off.

Nervously, she looked around, listening for the sound of any animal activity. Would a fisher attack a human?

It was with relief that she let herself into the quiet of The Maples. A few cats came to meet her: Bob, Mother and Jay, and Min Min. Lightning came too but stayed at the far end of the living room. Gerry took a big glass of water and sat at the room's table. She pulled her not yet completed first draft of *The Cake-Jumping Cats of Dibble* over and re-entered its world, where a cat was queen, her courtiers were dogs, her human friends compliant, and it was always time for cake and tea.

"How are the cakes coming?" Atholfass, Queen of Dibble, in the province of Fasswassenbassett asked her good friend Latooth Élonga, a not-quite-yet-elderly author who was paying an extended visit at the Queen's castle.

Latooth smiled modestly and urged the Queen and her courtiers to follow her to the kitchen. The hem of her dark grey dress drooped at the back and her shoes were worn down, but she walked like a lady. Proudly she displayed her latest creations.

They gazed, awestruck, at a stack of at least twenty meringue disks that diminished in size from the bottom layers to the top, sandwiched together with whipped cream. "Adjustable," murmured Latooth.

Queen Atholfass jumped onto the table and sniffed the stack, licked a bit of cream from the edge of the plate. "Clever," she said, then did a double take as she came face to face with a pair of life-size white chocolate swans. "Tricky," she praised.

Next, she edged around an enormous treacle cake oozing syrup. "Sticky," quipped Max, Count Scarfnhatznmitz, a flamboyant border collie. This drew a stifled giggle from his cousin Tess, Lady Ponscomb, a black flat-coat retriever. The Queen glared at the dogs.

She strolled up to a Gâteau St. Honoré built of cream-filled puff pastry balls made to resemble a castle, the whole edifice held together by a delicate caramel syrup and decorated with spun sugar. "Fantastic," purred the Queen. "It looks like Castle Dibble."

"Yes, dear. Thank you, dear," beamed Latooth.

"Can we eat any of these?" drooled Max.

"Of course, dear. These are just samples. Of what jumps on the course might look like."

The little group relaxed at the kitchen table and planned what ought to happen next while Latooth cut into the treacle cake and Languida Fatiguée, a little girl somewhat related to Latooth, made a pot of tea.

Gerry got up and fetched another glass of water. Her headache receding, she planned the illustration for this bit of text. "A big long narrow table. Well, like this one." She imagined how much space each of the four cakes might take up and positioned her characters near them. "A long drawing that might run along the bottom of two facing pages."

She quickly sketched. The Queen sniffed the stack of meringues. Tess admired the white chocolate swans. Max's large ham-like tongue lapped at a bit of syrup running off the treacle cake's plate onto the edge of the table. Languida furtively removed one of the cream puffs from the lower part of Castle Dibble's wall, causing the structure to begin to collapse.

Oh, why couldn't life consist solely of these lovely moments when she lost herself in her work?

She stretched and noticed how quiet the house had become, except for the odd creak of ancient timber. A cat sneezed. She smiled and went to bed.

When she woke in the morning, her first thought wasn't of Dibble—its cats and courtiers, its cakes and endless tea parties—but of protecting the window in the house next door. She felt bad she'd forgotten do it earlier.

She'd set her alarm for seven, knowing she had to be out the door heading for the college by 12:15 at the latest. She reread the day's lecture as she drank her first coffee. "Historical context, Europe, blah, blah, Romantic period to realism, blah blah blah overview," she muttered. "Trends, movements, compare and contrast. Okay, I think that's all right. Bob, do you want to come with me and repair that window covering?"

The tuxedo cat rolled on the braided hearthrug. One of the grey tiger cats—Gerry thought it was Joe, but what happened happened so fast it was hard to tell—jumped on Bob. Joe's brothers, Winnie and Frank, jumped too, then their diminutive sidekick Ronald got involved. It was all friendly but it meant Bob shot off into the next room and Gerry went next door alone.

As she entered the long semi-circular driveway that swung behind the house, she saw freshly fallen snow had obliterated her and Bob's footprints across the lawn. And no one had cleared the driveway. She marched to the house's far side. But the nails stayed in her pocket and her hammer hung unused in her hand. Not only was the plywood protection on the ground under the window, but the window glass was shattered.

Gerry backed away and ran home to call the police. Perhaps if Bob had been there, he might have noticed, leading away from the window, tiny paw prints in the snow.

# PART 2

# SHRIKE

*A flutter. A flutter just at the edge of his vision. The grey cat made as if to turn his head, stopped. Pain. But the flutter.*

*He remembered the tree; he remembered looking down from his place in the window. In the house. He wondered if the old man was still asleep. Cold.*

*He remembered the feel of cold snow on the path behind the house. His paws twitched. But which house? He saw the way and followed it. White.*

*It hurt to trot but he kept going. He kept going under the gate and across the back of the house where he used to live with the many other cats. He looked down to the shore. No flutter.*

*But something had happened down there. He continued until he was almost directly under the tree. He looked up and then back toward his old house and saw himself sitting in a window high up under one of its gables.*

*But he didn't live there anymore. What was his name? He'd had a few. His mind became confused, his paws twitched again and he heard a low murmur. He turned his head and the thing was upon him.*

*Run. He must run. He shot diagonally across the snow-covered lawn. The hell with paths. He almost flew over the snow. He heard the thing behind him, scrabbling. It was fast but bigger so he must have the edge. Mustn't he?*

*He made it to the gate and shot under and through his own backyard to the base of the red-barked tree.*

*The hunter was stymied by the gate; didn't appear to like it, or was unable to fit under it. The cat watched from halfway up the tree, resting. Then the hunter seemed to make up its mind and quickly swarmed up and over the gate.*

*The cat spat and cursed the tree's smooth bark. No purchase unless he dug his claws well in and that slowed him. He desperately continued his climb.*

*He could hear the creature closing the gap. It was climbing the tree! No fair! shrieked the cat. Climbing trees was one of a cat's few defences against larger predators.*

*He made it to the height on the tree from where the ledge on the house beckoned. He leapt and was halfway through the squirrel hole when the creature behind him must have leapt too. He felt a searing pain down one side.*

*The murmur ceased. His paws stopped twitching.*

# 6

The police response to Gerry's call was underwhelming. No one called back, and after she'd fretted away the morning doing chores, getting ready to teach and peering out her kitchen window at the house next door, she had calmed herself down enough to realize why.

A broken window in an abandoned house in winter. Right. Like that mattered compared to car accidents, house fires and heart attacks, not to mention real criminal activities.

She phoned first Cathy to alert her and then Blaise. "But I'm sure we don't have to worry about break-ins," she reassured him. "It's because the house is empty."

"I read in the paper that its previous occupant just died. A woman. She was older than me. Over 100."

"That's encouraging." She sought to change the subject. "How's Graymalkin?"

"The drain is gone and they've stitched him up, but he's still full of drugs. They say he stirred yesterday. Cathy took me and I sat with him for a while, just talking and stroking his head." Blaise's voice caught in his throat. "His paws twitched but that was it."

"Well, Cathy says Dr. Morin is the best vet around here."

"Are your cats all right, Gerry?"

"Yes. But I'm not letting them outside unless I'm with them. Not that most of them want to go out in winter. Only Bob and sometimes the boys. You know: Winnie and his brothers."

"I know. And how is that nice young cousin of yours? What's his name? Doug's youngest."

"David? He's fine, I think. He goes to the same college where I'm teaching. You know—Ross Davidson. But it's a big place. I haven't seen him yet. Look, Blaise, I've got to get going. Bye bye."

She was hungry again but again, there was no time. She rushed to a fast-food place near the college, parked and ate in her car. Mm, she thought as she wolfed the breakfast: cheese, bacon and egg on an English muffin with a wodge of deep-fried potato. My car is going to start smelling like a restaurant.

As she savoured the salt and the fat, the big Cadillac she'd seen the foreign student from the college tour get out of pulled up. This time the car was driven by a scowling woman. A couple of frightened-looking girls got out and scuttled away. After the car left, the young man joined the girls. They all looked furtively around as a heated discussion erupted. Finally they dispersed. "Huh," Gerry remarked to the air as she gathered her garbage and her notes and set off for class. "I wonder what all that was about."

"Please put that phone away, Miss," Gerry warned the young girl at the back of the room. "I won't tell you again. You may keep your phones but not use them." The girl flushed, defiantly worked her thumbs for a few more seconds before realizing Gerry and most of her classmates were watching. She put it away, crossed her arms across her chest and slid down in her seat.

"Thank you," Gerry said calmly. The trick was not to appear intimidated. She returned to the painting they were viewing. "Now, we may find these works boring." Vernet's *The Battle of Friedland* was on the screen. Napoleon on horseback was surrounded by his generals and the captured and dead of his enemies. "Painted in 1835-ish, this is a fine example of history painting. Nothing wrong with it. Fine technique. Just, to us, not much emotion."

She clicked and Bonnat's *The Martyrdom of Saint Denis* appeared. "Boring or gross, depending how you look at it. Now, this was painted fifty years later and is another example of history painting, but done in a style called revival. Note the columns and costumes harking back to biblical times." She let them look for a moment. "I rather like the exposed sinews of the saint's neck where the skin has torn off. And look at how sharp the axe is. The painting is full of symbolism but we would say, again, not much emotion."

She clicked again. "Let's go back to the same period the Napoleonic work was done and see another war painting. This is Goya's *The Third of May 1808* painted in 1814. Now, we have maybe a rougher, less polished technique, but look at the face of the central character. Despair, bravery and fear are mixed there. The composition is simple. Soldiers on one side, prisoners on the other. The night sky is above both groups but a strong light illuminating the hero shows us who the artist admires. And we can relate to this human confrontation where possibly we don't relate to saints or emperors."

She clicked off the machine and turned on the lights. "Any questions?" One boy raised his hand. "Yes?"

"Is it true, Miss Coneybear, that you're a cartoonist?" She nodded. "Is it hard to get work?"

She thought for a moment. "I think we should confine ourselves to art history questions for now." She smiled. "Any art history questions? No? Okay. This is your homework." A collective groan filled the room. "Don't panic. Just read the chapter on history painting and compare in a short essay—one page will do—two paintings we did not cover today." She stepped down off the platform and approached the boy. "You are?"

"Jerry Pinsky."

"Another Gerry!"

"Jerry with a *J*."

"Are you a cartoonist too?" Gerry with a G asked.

"I fool around."

"Cool. I always doodled as a kid and took art in high school. Then in college I found my sense of humour creeping into my projects. That's when I knew I might be a cartoonist. Does that describe you?"

"Kind of. Only I like to draw superheroes."

"Ah. Sounds like your real interest might lie in comic books, not cartoons. But give yourself time to develop as an artist. That could change."

"Oh, I'm not in fine arts. I'm in engineering. This is an elective for me."

Gerry felt deflated. "Oh. Well. It's always good to have interests outside of your main area of study. Nice talking with you."

As the room emptied and Gerry packed her class materials away, she muttered, "Nobody is going into fine arts these days, you idiot, because they can't make a living." She remembered how precarious her existence had been after college. No work to speak of so she'd taken part-time secretarial jobs and worked at *Mug the Bug* in the rest of her time. The relief had been huge when Mug had found a home with one major paper and then been syndicated across the country in smaller ones. She'd quit her part-time job of the moment and plunged into the commercial art world, taking Mug around with her as her entry point.

"I was lucky. So lucky." She walked to the building that housed the administration offices and handed in a health form.

"Oh, Gerry, I'm glad I caught you." The harried administrator who'd hired her handed her a decal. "For your car. So you can park in the staff parking. Near the building."

Gerry looked at the decal in her hand. "There's staff parking?"

"Yeah. Just out that door. Saves walking time."

It certainly does, Gerry agreed, as, a refund for the original decal she'd purchased negotiated, she trudged through twilight to get to her car, as usual parked in almost the last row of the lot. She stuck the decal inside her windshield next to the first one and yawned. Teaching was exhausting. A cup of coffee and a nap was what she needed.

What she got when she arrived home was the sight of police cars and an ambulance alongside the road, and yellow tape around the empty house next door. She barely had time to feed the cats and clean the litter boxes before a knock came on the front door. A police officer stood there, looking polite but wary. Gerry assumed a similar mask.

The interview, conducted at her living room table, was a dance. The officer asked Gerry to describe events leading up to her call, while Gerry tried to guess why there could be all this fuss about a broken window.

"And were you wearing gloves when you pried off the window covering?"

"Yes."

"And did you remove your gloves when you were inside the house."

"Uh, I don't think so. But I may have done."

"And did you never think that you might be trespassing on private property?"

"I was thinking about Blaise's cat. Mr. Parminter's cat.

"And what made you think the cat could have entered a boarded-up house?"

"Well, he got out of his own house without Mr. Parminter knowing, and my cat, Bob—" Here, Bob, lying on the hearth rug, yawned, showing the officer his fearsome set of fangs. "Bob jumped up on the window box and kind of pulled at the plywood covering the window. He and Stup—I mean Graymalkin—are kind of pals and—well, not pals, more like arch enemies—" Gerry could feel the sweat forming in her armpits and beginning to run down her sides. She suddenly heard her words and realized how weird they must sound to the officer. She finished lamely. "I just thought Bob might be sensing Graymalkin inside the house. And I noticed a little hole low down near the foundation where a small animal might be able to get in. But, obviously, I wouldn't be able to fit in that way so—"

"So you broke in."

"I went back this morning to try and repair the window covering. The plywood was rotten and just peeled off." She brought the officer her coat and patted one pocket. "See? Nails. And then I phoned."

"Presumably you took a hammer as well," the officer commented drily.

"Yes. But not in my pocket." Gerry paused.

"Could I see the hammer?"

Nonplussed, Gerry walked to the back porch and presented the hammer. "Really, what's this about? Is…is someone dead over there?"

The officer took pity on her, or maybe she just didn't like cats. Several of Gerry's mob had begun slinking into the room, furtively sniffing the officer's legs. She shifted warily in her chair, and when Min Min put his paws on her thigh and mewed, she abruptly stood.

"He just wants you to pick him up," Gerry explained.

"Do you mind coming next door with me?" The officer returned the hammer to Gerry, then edged toward the front door.

"The side door is quicker," Gerry murmured, slipping on her coat.

She followed the officer onto the road. They slipped under the yellow scene-of-crime tape. Gerry felt for a moment that she was in a TV drama; that this couldn't really be happening. As they approached the house, she noticed the Christmas wreath was missing from the front door.

"You took your time," grunted another police officer guarding the entrance. Gerry's officer ignored him and ushered Gerry in, through the hallway, then blocked the doorway to the kitchen.

"You're going to see a body," she said calmly and stepped aside. Gerry took one step into the room and stopped.

Unlike her kitchen at The Maples, crammed along one of the short sides of the house, this kitchen was long and commanded a view of the lake from its many windows. There was room for a large table, even a sofa if one had wished. In the morning it would be a light and cheerful room. Now, in the early evening, it was dark and dusty, empty except for the shape in the body bag on the gurney.

As Gerry approached the body, her officer unzipped the bag a bit. It was a man's face, elderly but not old. For some reason Gerry felt relieved and audibly let out a breath. The officer became alert. "Know him?"

"I think I do." The face, thin with a receding hairline, was calm. Gerry remembered that awful set expression from seeing her dead mother when she was a teenager and her father not so long ago. Peaceful and—absent. She felt her eyes fill and her face crumple.

"Try to think where you might have seen him," the officer urged gently.

Gerry blinked and wiped her tears. She looked again, tried to visualize the face alive with open eyes and first a smile, then a frown. The frown did it. "At Ross Davidson College. He drove a big old fancy car, dropped a kid off, a student—or some students. I forget. He almost ran me over in one of the crosswalks." She looked again. "Huh. Poor man. How did he die?"

The officer zipped up the bag, ignoring Gerry's question. "Got his name? Him or the students?"

"No, I'm sorry. I never met the man but one of the students and I exchanged a few words on a tour of the campus we both took on Monday. It was Tuesday morning when I was here looking for the cat and there was no body then. Besides, after that was when I saw him—the man—at college, just before one o'clock."

"And you're a student at Ross Davidson?"

"I—" Gerry drew herself up to her full but still diminutive height. "I am a teacher there. Art history." Then she wilted. "Only a part-time, last-minute substitute teacher."

The officer, a tall woman, smiled. "You seem very young, for a professor, I mean." An ambulance attendant stuck his head in the room. The officer nodded and he and another came in and wheeled the body out. Gerry noticed quite a lot of blood on the kitchen floor. Once again, she let out a big breath. "Your first dead body?" the officer queried quietly.

"No. Sadly, not." As they exited the house, Gerry asked, "I'm sorry. I must not have been paying attention. What's your name again?"

"Leduc. Isabelle. We may need to talk to you another time."

"You know where to find me. Me and my nineteen cats!" She laughed wildly, then, horrified, choked the laugh short. "Sorry," she muttered and skittered away.

Once home, she made a pot of tea and tried to get her bearings. Thursday. It was Thursday evening. What time? Six o'clock. Okay. When had she last eaten? She remembered the yummy lunch eaten in her car. That felt like days ago. Okay. She should eat again.

She walked into the kitchen and put two slices of whole wheat bread into the toaster. "Peanut butter," she mumbled, and got it, butter and milk from the fridge. She stared at the calendar. Tomorrow was Friday and looked free. Good. Then Saturday and she was going to Bea and Cece's for supper. Nice. And Sunday around four she was to pick up Prudence at the airport. The toast popped. She raised her eyebrows. "Oh—my—God! What's Prudence going to say?"

# 7

Friday morning, Gerry hid inside.

The crime-scene tape next door, flapping in the breeze, made traffic slow while people peered at the long white house. And word of the death must have spread through Lovering, for a greater number of cars than usual paraded deliberately by. Some even had the audacity to pull into Gerry's driveway behind the Mini, back out and return slowly the other way.

She made a fire in the living room, and ignoring the road, sat at her worktable facing the lake.

Sunlight slanted through bare trees to mingle on the snowy lawn with the trees' shadows. And the breeze made this play of light and dark shift. "How to indicate movement of light," she murmured and for half an hour, on a piece of paper, tried.

With a sigh, she put down her pencil and looked at planning the next two art history classes. Tuesday shouldn't be too hard. She'd get the kids to present their homework and discuss. That should wrap up history painting. Then on Thursday, they'd begin an in-depth look at symbolism. She read for a bit, making notes.

Her peace was disturbed by a quiet tap at the kitchen door. Cathy stood in the driveway with Prince Charles. He was wearing the red coat Gerry had given him for Christmas. Gerry smiled and opened the door. "Come in, you two."

Cathy replied, "Well, maybe just into the kitchen. Because it's so cold." Gerry quickly lifted the tub of cat kibble onto the counter and closed the door into the living room. Charles began a nasal inspection of the porch and kitchen, snuffling and scoring crumbs and bits of leftover cat food.

Cathy took off her gloves and breathed on her hands. "Isn't it terrible?" she commented, jerking her head in the direction of the house next door.

Gerry nodded. "I saw the body."

"No!" Her friend looked shocked. "Was it—gory?"

"No. Some blood on the floor. He was in the bag they put them in. Did you know him?"

"Nolan Shrike? No. But I know his face, if that's what you mean. And his wife's. Carolyn? Elizabeth? Seen them in town."

"Oh, the poor woman," Gerry offered.

"Mm. Anyway, I wondered if you're free, if you want to do that lunch today?"

"Oh. Sure, Cathy." Gerry checked the clock on the stove. "Let's say in about an hour-and-a-half? I'll pick you up." She bent over to bid farewell to the prince, now sitting looking up at the women. "And Charles, you look very smart in your coat." She scrunched the loose skin between his ears and his eyes half closed.

When her friends had gone, Gerry added "dog cookies" to the shopping list magnetized to the fridge. After all, she thought, I know two dogs now. Then she added "people cookies" and went off to shower.

She picked up Cathy just before one and they drove into Lovering. As it was Gerry treating Cathy, Gerry let Cathy choose the restaurant. She selected the Tiny Place, a new and, well, tiny restaurant that had recently opened.

"I heard they do different kinds of grilled cheese sandwiches at lunch. I'm curious," Cathy offered as justification for her choice.

"Great. I love them. Well, who doesn't?"

They entered the restaurant, two little rooms carved out of the side of the same building that housed the grocery store. A few small tables and chairs were crammed together in one; the kitchen was in the other. "Cute," Gerry said, and scanned the menu. After they'd ordered, she lowered her voice and asked, "Did you hear anything about Nolan Shrike? I mean besides his name. Which I didn't know. Why was he in that empty house?"

"Well." Cathy leaned forward. "They're originally British. Came here about thirty years ago. He worked as a security advisor—pretty vague-sounding job—and she raised their children. They're gone now, the children. One's in Toronto and one's in Vancouver, I think." She sat up as their waiter approached with two glasses of white wine.

"Compliments of the management," he said. "It's a promotion to say thank you for coming to our restaurant."

"Oh, how nice!" Cathy beamed at him. The friends toasted each other. "And it's not the cheap stuff, either," Cathy added, savouring the cold liquid.

"Isn't it? I can't tell." Gerry took a refreshing sip and smacked her lips. "It's nice, though. You were saying?"

"Yes. Well. After he retired, Mr. Shrike, Nolan, set up a company, looking after empty buildings. You know, if you went away for the winter, he'd check your house. Or if it's completely untenanted, like the house next to you."

"Oh, a caretaker. So he'd have had keys to the front and back doors."

Cathy nodded. "He mustn't have been making very much money though, because Mrs. Shrike takes in student boarders. Foreign students."

It was Gerry's turn to nod. "I saw him and then her, on a different day, dropping some kids off at Ross Davidson. Driving a big old car."

"Well, that's it. That car must be at least twenty-five years old. You'd think if they had any money, they'd replace it."

Their sandwiches arrived. Cathy's oozed with creamy Brie and caramelized onions contrasting with thin crisp slices of pear. Though she'd been tempted by the Reuben—smoked meat, Swiss and sauerkraut—Gerry had gone for the tried and true combination of roast beef and Danish blue. The sandwiches came with fresh fruit and home-fried potatoes.

Except for some "mmms," there was silence at their table for a few minutes. Then Gerry spoke. "Hear anything about how he died?"

Cathy swallowed and shook her head.

Gerry said slowly, "As far as I could tell, he wasn't slugged in the head."

"Right. You saw the body."

Gerry nodded and pushed her plate away. "Boy, that was good. Yeah, the police questioned me at my place—because I phoned about that broken window, remember? Then they took me to view him. It. It was in the kitchen covered up to the neck. Do you want dessert?"

Cathy, not one to worry about her figure, beckoned to the waiter. "What dessert do you have that would complement white wine and grilled cheese?" When he looked perplexed, Cathy laughed and said, "I'm just teasing you."

He smiled. "I don't know if it's complementary, but the apple pie is good."

"We'll have two of those. With ice cream. Okay, Gerry?"

"Great. And coffee, please."

The two settled back in happy anticipation. Two more women entered the restaurant and their heads were soon in close proximity as information of some kind was relayed.

"Probably talking about the same thing we were," Gerry said out of the corner of her mouth.

They overheard, "...in the neck. So did he die right away or linger, do you think?" What the other woman said was indistinguishable. Gerry and Cathy exchanged a shamefaced look.

"Someone died," Gerry said soberly.

"Someone was widowed," Cathy added.

"Let's talk about something else," Gerry suggested.

"Let's. Let's talk about Jean-Louis."

So they chatted their way through dessert, Gerry paid, and they walked through to the grocery store. Gerry was looking doubtfully from broccoli to cauliflower—people really should eat vegetables, an inner voice admonished—and Cathy was peering at berries, when a voice at Gerry's elbow said, "How you doing?"

She turned and beheld Doug Shapland, her part-time handyman/gardener, inherited from her Aunt Maggie along with Prudence, the house and the cats. He was related to Gerry by blood, but distantly, and, rather more closely, by marriage, or rather, ex-marriage to her cousin Margaret. She hadn't seen him since the successful and, at the same time, disastrous dinner party she'd given earlier that month. "How are you?" she replied. "How's life as a full-time dad?"

As his ex-wife had recently entered a mental institution, Doug had moved back into their family home to care for the couple's three young adult sons: James, Geoff Jr. and David. Gerry looked around for Cathy but she'd disappeared. As Doug spoke she studied him. Not too tall, of slight build, with brown hair and eyes.

He smiled his shy smile and her heart warmed. "Life is good. The boys are getting used to having me around again. The kitten you gave us is fun to play with. But her name changed from Dee to Didi. She's taken to David in a big way so we put the litter box downstairs next to his room and she sleeps with him."

"Aw. I'm glad. You curling? I mean—" She stopped, remembering his team had lost two of its five players. One of the men had died; the other was awaiting trial.

A shadow covered his face. "Yeah. We found replacements all right. Are you busy drawing your cartoons?"

"Mm hm. And teaching. Just one course. At Ross Davidson. Will I see David there?"

"You should. Geoff Jr. goes there too. Second year. I'm just not sure how much actual studying and how much goofing off playing cards goes on." They both laughed.

"Oh, Doug, you'd know this. What causes witch's broom on trees? I saw some on the pines up in the woods. You know, the plantation Uncle Geoff put in."

"It happens when the plant is stressed. The way the pines are crowded together—monoculture—with no other different species growing near them—is highly stressful. They're vulnerable to disease, to pests, to fungus. The brooms on the pines are caused by a rust fungus, I think. The tree thinks it's dying so grows a miniature version of itself on a branch."

"I knew you'd know. You're a walking horticultural encyclopaedia."

Cathy arrived, bearing blueberries, and kissed Doug on both cheeks. Oh, I should have done that, Gerry realized. But the memory of their more romantic kissing one night in Gerry's car after Christmas, followed by Doug's present seeming lack of interest, had held her back.

"Well, I'll be seeing you," he said.

"Bye, Doug," both women replied.

"He's so nice now he's not drinking," Cathy said. "Gerry, I need to go back to the dairy section for whipped cream. You go line up."

Gerry dropped Cathy off at her house and returned home. She felt drowsy, so she fed the cats early and went for a nap. She dreamt that the cat Graymalkin was back living in her house but that now, instead of being solitary and unaffectionate, he was the most loving of companions, following her from room to room. She realized that the rooms were those of the upstairs of the empty house next door, and Gray wasn't following her but leading the way.

In one room he jumped up onto the windowsill and everywhere he stepped, a tiny witch's broom sprouted and grew.

She woke with a snort. "The wine, Bob, the wine. I'm not used to drinking at lunch." Well, not anymore, she thought, remembering plenty of wine-soaked afternoons spent with friends as an art student. "I used to be." Bob, sprawled splendidly on her bedside rug, blinked, as if to say, "Ah, youth."

Coffee was indicated. She put on a robe and went downstairs. Only five o'clock but dark outside. She inhaled the coffee's hazelnut vanilla aroma as she heated and frothed some milk. Bliss was a well-made cup of coffee taken at the appropriate moment. With some of the shortbread cookies she'd purchased. She made a fire and, as the cats gathered, drew the manuscript of *The Cake-Jumping Cats of Dibble* to her.

"Many responses to the posters, Tess?" asked Max.

She handed him a napkin for his treacly whiskers and replied, "A few."

"How many?" demanded the Queen.

"Six, Your Majesty."

"I will see them now." This was said haughtily. Atholfass sat up.

"Yes, Your Majesty." Tess ran out the kitchen door and returned with a little group of cats, mostly kittens, all very much awed by being in the presence of their Queen.

"Give them some cake," said Atholfass majestically, slowly looking them over. "They seem fit enough. You, boy, can you jump?"

The ginger-striped shorthair proved it, nervously reacting to the Queen's attention by going straight up. "Yes, Your Majesty," he squeaked. "We have good jumpers in our family."

"Good. Good. And what about you?" She turned suddenly to come nose-to-nose with a grey-striped female version of the first cat. The little thing dropped its piece of cake on the floor where Max made quick work of it. The kitten burst into tears.

"There, there," cooed Languida. "You oughtn't to be so mean to them," she scolded the Queen. "They're just babies."

"You forget yourself, Miss Fatiguée." And with that, the Queen stalked from the kitchen, tail high.

The three little drawings Gerry made for this bit of text showed first, Queen Atholfass inspecting the troops; second, the ginger cat up in the air; and third, the grey cat sprawled on its bum, weeping while Max gulped its chunk of cake.

As usual, she worked past hunger and, while the cauliflower she'd purchased languished in the fridge, settled for baked beans and toast and a cup of tea for her supper around eight. She switched to working on *Mug the Bug* and managed two strips. At one in the morning, she yawned and went to bed.

Saturday dawned dull but warmer. It began to snow and Gerry, chores done and caught up with her various projects, contemplated taking a day off. Should she drive across the ice bridge in search of the perfect french fry? But it had only been really cold again for a day or so. Maybe the ice wasn't quite hard enough yet. Besides, she could use some exercise.

After lunch—ham and cheese on a croissant liberally smeared with mayonnaise and hot mustard—she stepped outside, strapped on her snowshoes and crossed the road, passing along the lane between Andrew's and Cathy's two houses and so into the woods.

The fresh snow was fluffy and she soon settled into a rhythm. She turned onto the railway tracks until she came to the golf course and was trying to decide whether to go left and climb its slope or right to where more level fields beckoned, when she felt a blow to the centre of her back. She half fell forward. “What the—?” The blow was repeated on one of her arms, she rolled onto her back and saw her assailant.

# 8

"Harriet! You scared me! What are you doing out here? Where's Jean-Louis?" The big husky, unable to answer any of her questions, but joyful in her ignorance, danced around Gerry. "You know what? I bought dog cookies yesterday but I didn't know I was going to meet you. My pockets are empty."

Harriet forgave her, kissing her on the lips.

"Ech!" said Gerry and hastily got up. "No, but seriously, Harriet, where is Jean-Louis?" Gerry scanned the landscape in all directions. The dog certainly seemed alone.

And then he appeared, silently, on cross-country skies. In contrast to the first time they'd met when Harriet was in Gerry's backyard, he was wearing the dullest of colours—greys and creams—as if he wanted to blend in with his surroundings. "I see Harriet found you," he said quietly.

Mischievously, Gerry asked, "I hope you remembered your moisturizer today."

"What?" He looked blank for a moment, then said, "Ah, yes. I remember. We were discussing our skin care regimes at Cathy's house."

"Your regime. I don't have one."

"Wait until your thirties," he replied wisely. "But look at you—snowshoeing around the woods alone."

Gerry didn't know why, but she suddenly felt slightly, ever so slightly, menaced. "Don't you think it's safe?"

He shrugged. "Like most places, that depends. It is safe and it is not safe depending on who else is around." He smiled. "Today, with the brave Harriet bounding through the snow, I think it is safe."

"No snowmobiles, either," she commented.

"It's Saturday," he said. "They'll be along."

"You're probably right. I think I'll head home before they arrive. Goodbye, Jean-Louis. Goodbye, Harriet." And with a wave for one and a pat for the other, Gerry carefully reversed and went home the way she'd come. Now why did I retreat like that? she wondered.

She placed her snowshoes in her side porch and walked to Blaise's house. He answered her knock with tears running down his cheeks. "Oh, Blaise," she wailed. "Is it the cat? Is he—?"

He said yes, then shook his head and laughed. "Oh, Gerry. He's all right. It's just I miss him. The house is so empty."

"Let's have a cup of tea, Blaise, and you can tell me all about it." They went to the back of the house and Gerry made tea while Blaise sat in his recliner and talked.

The cat had had its surgery but was still sedated, as the less he moved, the better. Blaise had been to see him that day. The poor thing would raise his head briefly, then fall back into a doze. It would be quite some time before he'd be coming home, but the vet was hopeful.

They drank their tea and Gerry described being surprised by Harriet on the tracks, and her lunch with Cathy in the new restaurant the day before. Her friend fell asleep and Gerry let herself out.

Her own beasts flocked around her, mewing loudly when she entered the house. "Oh, come on now. I'm only fifteen minutes late." It was a quarter past four. She fed them, then went to change for supper.

On her way into Lovering, she stopped at the convenience store for a few purchases, then arrived at Bea and Cece's front door at a little after six.

"It's a good thing you're late, Gerry." Cece greeted her, holding a black and white kitten similar to Jay. It was struggling. "She wants to get out. Quick, close the door. Stop it, Cecilia."

He dropped the kitten and took Gerry's coat. "Bea had a bit of a disaster with her cake and we're running late."

"It's all right. I brought ice cream," Gerry replied.

"Don't look!" a voice cried from the kitchen. "It's just sad." Gerry went through. Bea covered her face with her apron and mock wept. Gerry looked at the cake, half of it upside down on a rack on the counter, half still in the pan, the centre mushy and underdone. The kitten ran in and jumped onto Bea's lap, rebounded off and dashed out of sight.

"What kind is it?" Gerry asked, interested in the cake's rich golden-brown colour, its spicy smell.

"It's supposed to be gingerbread."

"Oh, good. I brought French vanilla ice cream. We can eat around the raw bits." She bent to kiss Bea who lowered the apron, beamed and said, "What a good friend you are."

Cece appeared with a bottle of sherry. "Drink?"

"*We-ell*," Bea drawled like a southern belle, "*how verah civahlahzed. Ah thank you, sah*." She fluttered her eyelashes at her husband.

Gerry snickered. Cece took it all in stride. "What's new, Gerry?" They sat at the table. Bea wheeled over to the fridge and rummaged for snacks.

"Oh, you know. Became a college professor, Blaise's cat almost eaten by a wild animal, a dead body next door. Just another typical week at The Maples."

A thudding sound was heard coming down the stairs. The kitten, Cee, one of Gerry's, and sister to Jay and Dee, appeared. Unlike Jay, she couldn't really be considered a tuxedo cat, as her white patches were most of her underbelly and she had white stockings right up to her hips. Bea crooned, "Cecilia, darling, where have you been?"

The little cat mewed pitifully. Because of her habit of mewing loudly for no apparent reason, she'd been named Cecilia for an opera singer Bea was fond of. Or so Bea said. But was it a coincidence that Bea's husband's name was Cecil? "Probably just had to use her litter box," Cece remarked. "It's upstairs." Cecilia trotted over to Bea and jumped up.

"I'm her favourite because I'm usually sitting down," Bea laughed.

Gerry felt a slight shadow pass over the evening. Her friend's MS kept her in her wheelchair most days, with rare exceptions. Cecilia turned repeatedly and prodded Bea's lap with her little pin-like claws. "I'm afraid you'll have to serve, darling. I've been suborned."

Later, when the plate of roast chicken and mixed vegetables smothered in golden gravy was but a happy memory, Gerry went into detail about her week.

"I knew Nolan Shrike was dead, just not that you were involved," Cece said thoughtfully. "You say you pulled on the plywood but didn't smash the glass."

She nodded.

"So not exactly breaking but certainly entering. I don't see that you did any damage." As Gerry's lawyer as well as friend, he was thinking aloud. "Except for trespass. Which doesn't mean much these days."

Gerry, her mouth full of fragrant cake and ice cream, opened her eyes wide and swallowed. "Do you think I'm in trouble?"

"Nonsense," Bea reassured. "You were looking for a cat for an elderly neighbour. Besides, you're a citizen in good standing and that still counts for something." She was feeding Cecilia bits of chicken from her plate.

"A citizen in good standing," Gerry murmured. "That makes me feel so old!"

"Well, you very nearly are old. I mean—twenty six!" Bea, cruising through her fifties, sampling all the delights life in Lovering could offer, teased her friend.

"Not for a few more weeks," Gerry replied defiantly. "When does youth end, exactly?"

Cece jerked his head towards his wife, who was letting the kitten in her lap lick melted ice cream off her plate. "For some of us, never." He served the coffee.

Bea beamed. "What a nice well-trained husband I've got. Don't you agree, Gerry?"

Gerry grinned. These two were one of the few advertisements in favour of marriage in her little circle. Everybody else was either divorced or seemed to bitterly resent their partner. And the singletons like her, like Cathy, like Prudence, appeared genuinely more content. Just—alone.

"Cathy tells me," Bea began archly, "that you seemed to get along quite well with the handsome Mr. Thibeault at her place the other night."

"He is handsome," Gerry agreed.

"But a ski instructor," Cece scoffed. "I mean, come on."

"I know, right?" Gerry agreed. "And he's in his thirties. Though he seems very intelligent. How can he earn a living just by teaching skiing? I mean: what about in summer? He says he works as a trainer but how much can you earn doing that?"

"Maybe his family is rich," Bea suggested.

"Yeah, maybe. But apart from that, there's something not quite right. About him or his situation. I don't know."

"He does live directly across from the empty house," Bea contributed.

"And I live next door to it but I'm not involved in the death!"

Bea sighed. "Okay, okay. You're defending him but he's not quite right. You're not in love."

"Well, but, I am," Gerry said, with a glint in her eye.

Both Cece and Bea reacted. "What!?"

"With his dog!" They laughed. "She's this gorgeous blond husky named Harriet. Lovely, friendly. What if it turns out I'm more of a dog person? And here I am stuck with nineteen cats!"

Cece, the lawyer, offered consolation. "Your Aunt Maggie's will stipulated you only had to keep the cats for five years. She gave you a way out."

Gerry considered the cats: their attachment to their home; their little funny faces. "Oh, like I'd just kick them all out," she muttered.

"No, but, you could be more strict about not adopting any more in the future." Cece coughed. "A natural attrition will occur."

"I gave away the kittens!" Gerry protested.

"All of them?" Cece eyed her coolly.

"Well, no. You got one, and Doug, and my student Judith Parsley. And I gave one to Betty Parsley's kids." (Betty Parsley had been murdered around Christmas time, leaving four teenage children.) "I kept Jay because she reminds me of Bob and, well, Mother, the big marmalade, needs someone to mother. She's the one that brought the kittens home in the first place."

"How many of the cats are elderly, Gerry?" Bea asked.

Gerry considered. "Ah, Min Min, Harley and Kitty-Cat are over fifteen. That's elderly for a cat, isn't it? And Cocoon is, I think, fourteen. Oh, but I don't want anybody to die!"

"Nobody wants anybody to die," Bea said briskly. "It just happens. And dogs don't even live as long as cats. Ten, twelve years and that's it."

"I'm going to have quite a pet cemetery at The Maples before I'm done," Gerry commented drily. A wave of sleepiness washed over her. "Listen, I've been pushing hard with work and snowshoeing, which I'm not used to. I'm going to have an early night."

"Good idea," her hostess agreed, following her to the door, Cecilia clinging to her mistress's lap. Gerry laughed at the sight.

"You guys," she said affectionately as she stooped to kiss Bea and stretched up to kiss Cece.

He asked, "Have you thought any more about making a will, Gerry?"

She started. "Oh. No, actually. I don't know who I should leave the house to."

"Well, when you're ready, let me know."

She nodded and stepped out into the cold night. That, and Cece's query, woke her up, as did scraping the car's windows while the heater defrosted its frozen interior.

Who could she leave The Maples and all Aunt Maggie's cats to? Prudence? Prudence seemed happy with her own little cottage and didn't own any pets. Andrew? He'd doubtless enjoy doing up The Maples, bringing to it his interior designer's expertise. Andrew was a possibility. Certainly not Margaret, who was dangerous, or Aunt Mary, who was cruel. Gerry shuddered, thinking what Aunt Mary would do about the cats. At least she could trust Andrew to be compassionate.

The temperature must have briefly risen that day, then dropped again at night. A thin layer of ice coating the road made her drive carefully. She was glad of her snow tires. Everyone had advised her to invest in good ones. It's a whole other way of life out here, she thought, contrasting how, in Toronto after a late night with friends, a cab would be called. Anyway, in Toronto, winter didn't seem to make much of an appearance, probably due to the warming influence of vast Lake Ontario.

She'd just passed St. Anne's Church and was beginning the small descent toward her house when something low to the ground streaked across the road followed by Harriet the husky. Gerry hit her brakes, the car lurched to the right and off the road. She felt it tilt as it sank into the ditch. Gingerly, she climbed out.

"Harriet! Where have you gotten to? Harriet!" Jean-Louis, wielding a large flashlight, found Gerry standing at the end of his driveway. "What happened?"

"Harriet chased something across the road so I braked. And slid. As you see, I'm stuck."

"My apologies, Gerry. I let her out for a pee and suddenly she took off. I will pay for a tow truck. Let me just catch my bad dog and I'll call for one."

But there was no need for catching as the bad dog came bounding up, grinning happily, tail wagging, huge ears flattened, a seductive grin on her face. Gerry hugged her as she jumped up. "I'm so glad I didn't hit her." Harriet licked her chin. "I wonder if she was chasing the animal that savaged my neighbour's cat. Have you met him?"

"Who? The neighbour or the cat? Or the savage animal? Harriet, don't jump," Jean-Louis said somewhat brusquely. "I'm supposed to be training her but sometimes—all right, good dog. Good dog. Harriet, heel." To Gerry's amazement, Harriet did. "Come to my place. We'll call for a tow."

They edged around Gerry's car, its nose in the ditch, its rear in Jean-Louis's driveway, and walked toward his cottage. It was quiet. Ice and snow crunched under their boots. "Who clears your driveway?" she asked.

"The Hudsons," he replied.

She looked up at the sky and a small "ah" escaped her lips. The stars in their beauty glittered over their heads. She dropped her gaze to his face. The steam from their breath mingled.

He began, "Gerry, I—" She grabbed his arm and pointed.

A fox, trotting across the field that abutted the driveway, stopped, suddenly aware of them. Harriet, happily snuffling for rabbits in the hedge on the drive's other side, didn't see it. As they watched, the fox decided they were harmless and trotted on its way.

"Beautiful," Gerry said softly.

"Very," Jean-Louis agreed, but whether he was looking at the fox or somewhere else, only Harriet saw. Before they entered the little old farmhouse, Gerry noticed what looked like a snowmobile under a tarp beside a woodpile.

She nodded toward it. "You ever use it?"

"Not really. It came with the house. I prefer to get some exercise when I go into the woods." Inside, Jean-Louis phoned for a tow and made cocoa. He held up a bottle of brandy. "Why not?" Gerry agreed. "But just a tablespoon. Otherwise I won't be able to taste the chocolate."

She looked around appreciatively. The farmhouse was completely wood finished inside and had a wood stove in its one ground-floor room—a kitchen-*cum*-living room. Jean-Louis bent and threw in a couple of logs.

"Fantastic heat," she said, holding her hands out to it.

"Much more efficient than a fireplace," he said briskly.

"Huh. I did not know that," she admitted.

"Radiant heat. With an open fire, much of the heat goes up the chimney. You have a fireplace?" She nodded. "You should get one of these. You just put it on the hearth and its chimney pipe goes inside your brick chimney."

"But I love the open fire."

He swung open the door of the wood stove and placed a screen over the opening. "Tada! You can also get one with a glass window."

"Wow!" Harriet came over and lay down with a sigh in front of the flames. Gerry rubbed her tummy with a foot. "Cozy. I wonder how much it costs."

He rearranged the logs with a poker and replaced the screen. "Not too much, I think. Buy a wood stove for a couple of thousand, then the labour of fitting the pipe. You'll use less wood. Pays for itself in a few years."

Both their heads jerked toward a window where the revolving light of the tow truck pulsed. Gerry jumped to her feet. "No, Harriet," Jean-Louis remonstrated. "You stay here."

"Thanks for the hot chocolate, Jean-Louis," Gerry said.

"You're welcome. And call me J-L, eh?"

The tow truck made quick work of hauling out the Mini, which appeared intact. Gerry drove it the few hundred feet to her driveway and let herself into the house with relief. Energy drained, she fell quickly asleep.

Bob's whiskers tickled her face. She pretended to be still unconscious and felt the smooth pads of one of his paws tapping her cheek. When he got to her eye, she couldn't help herself and put up a hand. "You win, Bob," she groaned and sat up.

The promise of last night's clear starry sky had been fulfilled: it was a sunny day. Gerry yawned. She trudged downstairs and did the usual chores, then took her coffee upstairs, ostensibly to get dressed. But bed proved too inviting and she crawled back in. She reached for her book, *The Darling Buds of May* by H. E. Bates, first published in 1958. Reading it was like visiting another planet.

Set in the fifties in England's agricultural heartland in summer, the book pulsated with the lives of the Larkin family and their neighbours, moving from one gorgeous meal or event to another. The contrast between the book's exuberant celebration of summer and the Canadian stoicism facing winter was almost painful. Gerry was hooked and had the four other books in the series piled on her bedside table waiting to be read.

As the tax inspector Mr. Charlton allowed himself to be led away by the luscious eldest daughter Mariette to explore the farm, the book slipped and Gerry fell back into sleep.

Harriet the husky leapt from tree to tree, gnashing her teeth on witch's brooms. Far below, a tiny Gerry called and called.

She woke. Someone was ringing the doorbell. "Argh! What now?" She hurried downstairs and peered at the female form hovering on the front porch. No one she knew and yet—she opened the door.

The woman looked her up and down with a dour expression on her face. Gerry, secure in her own house, albeit in a Winnie the Pooh robe and SpongeBob slippers, flushed and held her ground. "Yes?" she said, somewhat haughtily.

"Shrike," the woman announced. "Mrs. May I come in?" She was dressed completely in brown, her hair dyed the same colour. She was painfully thin. In her sixties, Gerry thought.

"Um, yes," Gerry replied. "I was napping. My car got stuck in a ditch last night…" She let her voice trail off. Mrs. Shrike was obviously not listening. She'd entered the foyer eagerly, looked around with a sharp appraising eye.

"Very nice house," she said with an English accent like the one BBC newscasters used. "Very nice things." She lifted a vase that sat on the hall table and Gerry could have sworn she struggled not to turn it over to look for a mark.

"Will you have tea?" she asked doubtfully, adding, "I didn't know your husband but I'm sorry for your loss." She wondered, why is she here?

Mrs. Shrike peeled off brown gloves and removed a brown beret. "That would be very nice." Gerry sat her in a rocking chair by the living room hearth, put on the kettle and took the other rocker. The cats, alerted to the presence of a new person, drifted by one by one, carefully smelling the guest. Only a few—Bob, the boys, Harley and Kitty-Cat—remained in the room after that and (or was Gerry imagining it?) they remained uncharacteristically alert, staring at Mrs. Shrike from unblinking eyes.

The woman seemed not to notice them, except to say as she accepted a cup of tea, "I heard you had a lot of cats. More of a dog person, myself." She refused the shortbread Gerry offered her.

Gerry, hungry after her nap, munched away, again noticing Mrs. Shrike's thinness and trying to feel pity.

"You're wondering why I'm here, I suppose."

Gerry nodded. Mrs. Shrike watched Gerry for a few seconds. Suddenly, Gerry knew how the mouse felt just before the cat pounces. She took another cookie.

"I understand you entered the house where my husband, where Nolan—" For the first time, a little of Mrs. Shrike's self-composure drained away and left her looking bewildered.

Gerry thought she should make some sort of statement. "I'm very sorry I went inside, but my elderly neighbour, Mr. Parminter, was worried about his missing cat and my cat, Bob there, seemed to be indicating we should try looking inside."

Bob stared at Mrs. Shrike. When Gerry said his name he turned his head, blinked at her as if to indicate, "You got that right," then refixated on the other woman. Gerry continued. "I also saw a little hole at the bottom of the rear wall, near the back door, and thought the cat might have..." She let her voice trail off.

Mrs. Shrike looked at the mantel where Gerry usually kept odds and ends along with a few ornaments. She changed the subject. "My husband Nolan came from the same part of England as many of the other original families of Lovering."

"He came from Devon?" a puzzled Gerry asked.

"Devon. Yes. He was even related to some Parsleys back there."

"Everybody is," Gerry remarked absently.

"What do you mean?" Mrs. Shrike replied angrily, two spots of colour appearing on her lean cheeks.

"Eh? Nothing. I'm related to some Parsleys myself. There are a lot of them."

Mrs. Shrike seemed satisfied that no offence had been meant and calmed down. "I was trying to explain that although we are relatively new arrivals, we have some family connections. People can be rude to newcomers."

Gerry had a thought that "people" were more likely to be put off by unpleasant manners and behaviours, but resisted sharing it. "More tea?"

Mrs. Shrike held out her cup. She took it plain, of course. She sighed. "Nolan should have taken Sharp with him. He might have given warning."

Gerry assumed Sharp to be an assistant and waited for further details.

"Sharp is devastated," Mrs. Shrike continued. "Lies with his nose on Nolan's boots, waiting to go for a walk in the woo—" She broke off and looked nervously at Gerry, who couldn't help picturing an imaginary employee lying on his dead boss's boots, desolate with loss.

"Ah. I see. The poor dog," she hazarded. "What kind of dog?"

"A foxhound," Mrs. Shrike sniffed. "Very good nose. Loves to run."

"Don't all dogs love to run?" Gerry replied pleasantly, forgetting about Prince Charles and thinking instead of Harriet. "I have a friend—"

Mrs. Shrike cut her off by standing. "So you didn't notice anything? Anything odd in the house when you entered?"

Ah ha! thought Gerry. The real reason for this visit. She truthfully answered, "No, nothing. Except—why was there a wreath on the door of an empty house? It's not there now—"

"Oh." Mrs. Shrike gave a half-laugh. "That was my idea. To camouflage the house's vacancy. Put a bow on it," she said rather bitterly, "and no one will notice. Perhaps it blew away. That reminds me, the old lady just died in a nursing home."

"Oh?" Gerry said, then slowly added, "I'm beginning to have a memory of someone very old living over there when I was a child."

"She was more than 100."

"Yes, I had heard that," Gerry said politely, walking her to the front door. She hardly noticed that the six cats accompanied them, arranging themselves on the stairs and observing. "I did see you and Mr. Shrike once each before, you know." Mrs. Shrike, pulling on her brown gloves, stiffened. "At the college. Dropping off your students. I teach part-time there."

Mrs. Shrike relaxed, if such a tense figure could be said to ever relax. "Oh. Well, you'll probably see me there again. One of these days. Thank you for the tea."

Gerry looked through the sheer fabric that curtained the windows either side of her front door. There was the big Cadillac—midnight blue—and, sitting in the passenger seat gazing right at her, was a black, white and tan dog. Sharp. She looked over her shoulder as the grandfather clock sounded the hour. The time registered. "Aagh!' she shouted as she rushed upstairs, scattering cats, who (one would have thought) must be getting used to these sudden alarms.

# 9

"And you wouldn't believe the price of a can of tuna. Or a bag of pasta. I had to visit the bank every couple of days just to get enough money to buy groceries."

Prudence paused for breath and Gerry cast a quick quizzical look at her friend and part-time housekeeper. Apart from a slight tan, Prudence's narrow face and grey hair worn in a small bun seemed unchanged.

"Didn't get to talk to people much, did you?"

Prudence laughed. "Have I been chattering? Sorry. No. I spoke with the waitresses and sometimes other guests. But you know couples want to be alone together when they're on vacation. Now, if there'd been another single lady with me—"

"Do you need to buy any groceries on the way home?" Gerry asked innocently.

"No. I'll make do with what I can borrow from Rita and Charlie."

Gerry, who knew Prudence's neighbours had stocked her fridge for her now that her storm-damaged cottage was repaired, smiled. "Do you want to work at my place tomorrow? Or leave it until Thursday?"

Prudence replied quickly, "Oh, I'll work. I bet your place needs it," she added slyly.

"You would win your bet." Gerry took the exit off the highway and turned onto the river road.

Prudence sighed. "Now I feel like I'm home."

The Lake of Two Mountains spread out to their right. Sun shone on its frozen surface where people were pursuing winter sports. Some skied while others skated. A little further along, a miniature village of tiny huts, each with a car or snowmobile parked at its door, showed the ice fishermen were in residence.

"What do they catch?" Gerry asked.

"Perch, I think."

"Good to eat?"

"Awfully small, most of them. Some people think ice fishing is just an excuse to drink beer."

Gerry laughed. The big bay disappeared as the road curved left. They entered the outskirts of Lovering. Prudence sighed again.

"Tired?"

"Mm."

"Was it nice there? In St. Lucia?"

"You would love it. Flowers everywhere, birds, tiny lizards hanging on the walls. The hotel only had five apartments. I had a big living room–dining room–kitchen with a balcony looking at the beach and the Grand Pitons—those are the two volcanic domes that are in every ad for St. Lucia—and the bedroom in the back with air conditioning. The restaurant downstairs was a big open area ten feet from the beach, with tables at one end and loungers at the other. I must have swum five times a day."

"It sounds fantastic." They turned onto Prudence's road.

"It was. And, Gerry, would you believe it? There was a cat, a white one, a female. Every day she'd somehow climb onto my balcony." Prudence looked guilty. "I fed her milk and canned tuna."

Gerry laughed. "Couldn't get away from cats, eh?"

Prudence continued. "Then she'd find me after I swam and sit on my lap on the lounger in the sun."

The car bumped over the tracks and pulled into her driveway. The small white cottage was restored to its former state. "I can hardly believe I'm going to sleep here again. It's been a month," its owner said.

"Well, I hope you sleep well," Gerry replied. "See you tomorrow."

Before she got out, Prudence sniffed. "You know this car smells like french fries."

Gerry grinned sheepishly. "Haven't been doing much cooking."

"On holiday," Prudence teased. "Like me. See you."

Back at her house, Gerry fed the teeming throng. Their supper was late and they were upset. "It'll be worth it tomorrow, cats. Your old friend is coming back." She made a fire, got her book and enjoyed her evening.

The next day Gerry and Prudence returned to their routine. Gerry picked Prudence up and made the reluctant woman drive. She needed the practice if she was ever going to get her licence.

Prudence took one look at the mess Gerry and nineteen cats had made in one week, rolled up her sleeves and got to work. Likewise, Gerry, thanking the foresight that had made her prepare two art history classes ahead, was able to concentrate on *Mug the Bug* and got two strips done. She and Prudence ate their lunches separately, but took a mutual break around three for coffee. Min Min was lifted onto Prudence's lap while, blinking contentedly, Jay sat on Gerry. Bob lay on his back on the hearthrug, displaying his three white triangles.

"You heard about Mr. Shrike?" Gerry asked, offering Prudence a store-bought shortbread cookie.

She looked at the cookies with disdain before taking one. "I'm away one week and you forget to bake?"

"Hey, I was busy! But I went up by the sugar shack and that reminded me: wasn't there a wonderful maple pie Aunt Maggie used to make? Am I right?"

"Yes. Pecan maple. I have the recipe if you want it. Are you changing the subject?"

"Trying to. Is it working?"

"No. Baking should be a pleasure for the cook as well as those eating her desserts."

"Well, I was three days at the college, then there was the murder."

"I heard." Prudence dunked the cookie and reluctantly ate some. "Rita had me over for supper last night. I'm all caught up."

"Do you know the wife?"

"Tall, thin, sour, dresses in brown a lot? Yeah. I've seen her around. She takes in students, I think."

"Why would someone wear nothing but brown?"

"Maybe she thinks she's still a Brownie," sniffed Prudence. "In uniform."

"A Brownie uniform?" asked Gerry, remembering only a frequently misplaced white and orange tie, added to whatever clothes she'd worn that day to school.

"In my day, Brownies wore a brown uniform. A brown long-sleeved shirt, brown skirt, brown knee socks, brown shoes which you had to polish before every meeting, a brown beret and a brown tie."

"That's a bit depressing. Were you supposed to blend in with the earth, or what?"

Prudence munched a second cookie. "That's exactly right. Brownies are helpful fairies who do good deeds for people. I don't remember doing helpful deeds so much as learning housekeeping skills. We did also camp and do orienteering, so it wasn't completely sexist. I quite liked being in a tent with a group of girls."

"I never went to camp. We did field trips out of Toronto to look at birds and habitats—stuff like that. It was fun—for a while. Mrs. Shrike doesn't seem to be one for good deeds, unless taking in foreign students counts. I imagine she gets paid for that?"

"I presume so. Anyway, what's her husband getting knifed got to do with her students?"

"He was knifed?"

"Rita said his throat was cut."

"I didn't know that. The bag was zipped up to his throat." Gerry gulped as she remembered the cold white face and was glad she hadn't had to see the wound. She stroked little Jay and shivered. "I hope it was fast."

Prudence nodded then looked at her pityingly. "You mean I'm back one day and I know more about this murder than you?"

Gerry made a face. "Cathy didn't know. Neither did Cece or Bea. And Jean-Louis is an outsider." She realized as soon as she'd said his name, she'd made a mistake. A slow flush crept from her neck to her cheeks.

"Rita's nephew is one of the paramedics who answered the call," Prudence replied smugly. "Jean-Louis, eh? What's his family name?"

"Thibeault," Gerry replied meekly.

Prudence considered. "There are Thibeaults here."

"I got the impression he's from north of Montreal. I don't know why. Maybe because he's a ski instructor, I assumed he'd be from the Laurentians."

"A ski instructor! What's he doing here?"

"What do you mean? He's working at Royal Mountain."

"Nothing against Royal Mountain, but it's small and they usually hire locals to teach there. Huh."

Gerry shrugged. "He said he'd teach me cross-country skiing. Here. In the woods."

"What's to teach? You just strap them on and go. You probably have some in the shed. Look in the rafters where the canoe is. You might have to buy boots though." She had shouted the last sentence as Gerry was up and out the door.

Bob skittered through the kitchen and eased out after her. "Maybe you should stay inside, Bob, until we know more about this fisher or whatever it is." Bob had already cleared the asphalt parking pad and was heading onto the road when Gerry caught him. "Are you crazy? You might get run over!" He wriggled so hard, he escaped and charged up the slight rise that led to the house next door.

Gerry ran after him. He took the driveway that circled the back of the house. She ducked under the yellow crime-scene tape and saw a flicker of coloured lights in an upstairs window. "Bob!" she hissed, not wanting to attract attention if anyone was in the house. Bob disappeared around the far side of the house. She looked up at the window. There. A flicker of red, yellow, green. Almost as if—

She followed Bob's little footprints and groaned. Someone, or the wind, had lifted the plywood cover from the broken window. It lay on the snowy ground. She was in time to see Bob's tail whisk out of sight. "Oh, no, trespassing again," she muttered. Then she stiffened, one leg on the sill, realizing there might be someone up there where the lights were. Nolan Shrike's killer, perhaps.

But Bob!

"Crap," she said and climbed through. Broken glass and drifted snow mingled under her feet. I guess the police don't clean up crime scenes, she thought. I wonder who the owner is now the old lady is dead. A sudden angry meow from upstairs made her run.

She paused at the top of the stairs. The coloured glow was coming from one of the rooms overlooking the lake. She stepped to the door as Bob shot out of the room, his fluffed tail streaming behind him, looking as though he'd seen a ghost. She looked in.

A narrow metal bedframe, an old mattress, a small bureau. And, on the floor, unplugged, a string of Christmas lights. Not glowing.

Gerry took one scared look around, then retreated after Bob, who had already exited the house by the time she scrambled out over the windowsill. She caught up with him as he entered the thicket separating the two houses. “Okay, Bob. You go that way. I’m not struggling through all those burrs. I’m taking the road.”

They met back at Gerry’s house. Gerry took a quick peek in the shed, pulled down an old pair of wooden skis and poles from the rafters, and stuck them in the snow next to the kitchen door. “Prudence, Prudence, when I was outside, the Christmas lights in the empty house next door were flickering, but when I got into the room they were unplugged!”

Prudence looked up from the grocery list she was making. “What lights? And why would you go into that place again?”

“Bob zoomed in, ran upstairs, gave a terrible meow and zoomed right back out. I was in there for two minutes.”

“He probably accidentally unplugged the lights. Maybe he got a shock. Do you want tomatoes?”

“What? No. Yes. I suppose so. But who plugged them in in the first place? Eh? Eh?”

Prudence looked at Gerry with a wrinkled brow. “You’re not getting a bee in your bonnet about the house next door, are you?” she asked suspiciously. “Because I’ve had enough murder to last me a lifetime.”

“Blame him.” Gerry pointed at Bob now innocuously crouched in front of the tub of kibble under the kitchen table. “He’s led me there twice. And I can make my own grocery list, thank you very much.” She snatched it off the counter and read: milk, cream, butter, cheese, ham, croissants, bread, chicken, broccoli, pasta, sauce, cat litter x 3, cat tins x 19, kibble—large. “Oh. Apparently I can’t make my own list. Do I really need all that? Cripes. Thank you, Prudence. As usual, you restore order where there is chaos.”

“You’re welcome. You’ll learn. Oh, I almost forgot.” She rummaged in her purse. “Coffee. And a cocoa stick. From St.

Lucia." She beamed. "I had a wonderful, uneventful, warm time. Thank you for sending me."

"Aw," Gerry said. "You deserve it, Prudence. A cocoa stick. 'Makes cocoa tea,'" she read. "Good thing it comes with instructions. Thank you. I should drive you home. But you drive."

Gerry was tired. It was the end (almost) of a long week. The weather had warmed and that meant snow—lots of snow. She'd struggled to work on Tuesday, heard the kids' efforts at comparing one history painting to another, and struggled home. Wednesday she hunkered down, feeding the fire and planning the next bit of *The Cake-Jumping Cats of Dibble*, even giving thought to a possible conclusion.

This morning she'd had to shovel out behind her car herself—the Hudsons were late. She wondered if the driveway would be cleared when she got home. She waved at an excited Andrew when he climbed into a taxi for the airport, picked up Prudence, then drove to Lovering to do her errands. She dropped off an ad at the *Lovering Herald* for more students for the drawing lessons she would soon resume teaching at home and picked up the groceries Prudence had listed.

She'd been almost out of cat food and had herself been living off of canned beans and packets of soup mix, crackers and peanut butter without really noticing. The driveway was still not cleared when she got home. As usual, after unpacking her groceries and shouting goodbye to Prudence, she had to rush off to the college, but the slushy roads made even a little speeding impossible and she was taking her coat off as the last students trickled in.

Almost two hours later she thought, time to wrap it up and clicked the remote. Delacroix's *The Death of Sardanapalus* appeared. "Now, this may look like just another boring history painting—" Some of the class, those who were paying attention, snickered. "It was done in 1827. In terms of the techniques used to present the subject matter, it's pretty revolutionary for its time." She drew a line diagonally across the painting from the upper left to the lower right. "See how light along this line pulls the eye to the centre where the two or three distraught female figures are struggling? And the gorgeous red fabric flowing off the bed onto the floor? It's a terrible scene and the painter has used colour and light to render it, to express emotion." She added, "And it's huge—twelve-and-a-half feet by sixteen feet. Contrast in size and treatment to this one." She clicked.

"Chassériau's *The Toilet of Esther* done in 1841. Yes, very funny." More snickers had been heard. "Toilet refers to the act of personal grooming as well as an actual toilet, which I don't think they had back then. This tiny painting—eighteen by fourteen inches—is appropriately sized, don't you think? It's an intimate subject. How cool the skin looks, refreshed. The opposite to what we saw in the Delacroix. But similar in that light takes the central position in the work. We hardly see the figures of the servants to Esther's left and right." She put down the clicker and sighed. "Any questions?"

Jerry Pinsky waved at her. "Yes, Jerry?"

"Do we have homework this weekend?"

"Your homework consists of reading the section on symbolism in painting—" There commenced the noise of twenty people rising. Gerry raised her voice. "And—" Groans erupted as they realized she wasn't done. "And noting two ways symbolism was used in the nineteenth century. With examples. Two pages, minimum."

She beckoned Jerry to her as the rest of the class dispersed. He looked glum. "Why'd you ask about homework, Jerry? You got a big weekend planned?"

"Going skiing, Miss. At Royal Mountain. Three days. Me and my friends rented a chalet."

Gerry grinned. She could imagine what kind of shape he'd be in by Monday morning. What with all the "skiing." "I suggest you do the reading and make notes tonight. Then all you have to do next week is put it together."

"Good plan. If I do it."

"I know one of the instructors there, a Mr. Thibeault."

"I can ski, Miss. I won't be taking lessons."

"Oh. Okay, then. Have fun."

She shrugged into her coat and slogged through snow to her car to begin the ritual: wipe snow off the driver's door with her mitten, get in, start the car, retrieve the small broom from the trunk, clean off the car, stomp snow off her boots and finally get behind the wheel.

The staff parking lot was near a circular driveway where a steady stream of cars entered and hovered until they picked up their kids. Gerry noticed one monster car, taking up almost two car lengths, waiting and waiting. Mrs. Shrike. When the two girls finally arrived and opened the car doors, Gerry heard a stream of abusive language. She assumed abusive from the tone as the words were indecipherable. Except for two that hung in the air long after the Cadillac's doors had slammed shut and it had been angrily driven off. They were "Kill you!"

# 10

Gerry thought about those words all the long slow drive home. There had been an accident on the highway and three lanes had to merge into one. It was almost six when she got home.

She let herself into the kitchen expecting to find Prudence gone and a horde of famished cats. Prudence was gone but instead of hungry cats she found sleepy ones and a note. "When I saw you were late, I fed the cats and phoned Charlie for a lift home. Your supper is in the fridge. 400 degrees for twenty minutes. P."

Gerry looked in the fridge. Four tin-foil-covered pie plates were neatly stacked. She took one out and peeled back the foil. A quarter of a chicken, roasted; a baked potato, quartered; and a cup of broccoli, already cooked. A can of a popular BBQ chicken restaurant's gravy stood on the stove. Prudence is showing me how it's done, she thought.

Gerry turned on the oven and phoned Prudence. "You, you are the best! I just got in. Thanks, Prudence."

"All right, all right. It was easy. I just roasted everything but the broccoli while I was doing other stuff. Driving bad?"

"An accident. Terrible. Two cars and a truck. What are you doing this weekend?"

"Well, tomorrow I have another client in the morning. Then I'm going to visit Mother."

"Visit Mother" was code for consulting a medium named Mrs. Smith. Prudence had been seeing her about once a month for years. She added, "You want to come?"

"Aah." Gerry was taken aback. She had consulted Mrs. Smith in the past, but only when things were getting weird. They weren't weird now, were they? "Ah, no, I don't think so, Prudence. Thanks for asking me though."

"Okay. I just thought you might like to ask if any tall dark ski instructors were going to impact your life."

"Hah hah. He's not that tall. And no, I'm not curious. Does Mrs. Smith do romantic consulting?"

"All the time. That and contacting dead or missing people. So, I'll see you Monday at 8:30."

By now wonderful smells were seeping from the oven and cats were likewise beginning to oil their ways chicken-ward. Gerry heated up the gravy and sat at the table in the living room with a sigh of anticipation.

After she ate she felt she deserved a reward so reached for her pile of drawings and texts for her cake-jumping cat book. "Now, where was I?" she asked Jay, who was stalking a tray of paper clips. "And down you go."

Gerry gently scooped the playful kitten up into the air and onto the floor, tossing her a catnip mouse someone had left on the table. As Jay rolled from side to side, holding the mouse and raking it with her hind legs, Gerry turned to imaginary cats. The Queen had just stalked from the kitchen in a huff.

> "Whew," said Max. "You were lucky."
>
> "It's because she likes you, dear," added Latooth. "She appreciates how you've thrown yourself into the project."
>
> Languida grinned. "I have, haven't I? Thrown myself. Perhaps I'll become an honorary member of the Cake-Jumping Cats of Dibble."
>
> "You already are, dear. You already are."

Later that day, Queen Atholfass sat sunning herself in a window of the castle that overlooked the cake-jumping course. Her tail lazily flapped up and down. This meant she was thinking.

She watched Max and Languida introducing the cake-jumping team to the idea of jumping over something. For example, Languida had placed a large stone on a table and was jumping back and forth over it.

The members of the team yawned and began to groom.

Max then jumped not only over the rock but the table as well, landing on an embarrassed Lady Ponscomb who'd been observing.

Members of the team curled up and napped.

Right, thought the Queen, and hopped off her comfy ledge, stalked downstairs and onto the field. "Wake up," she hissed at the sleeping would-be cake-jumpers. "Wake up or die."

The young cats, hearing their Queen's angry voice, were all terrified attention.

"Follow me," she said, and proceeded to lead the youngsters up and over, around and down, through and to the end of the course. "And that," she panted, "is how it's done."

Gerry thought a few little sketches, done comic strip–style, would serve this section of the book, and roughed them out.

The first would include the Queen high up in the castle watching as the team composed itself for a nap and Max squashed Tess.

The second would show the Queen leading the team around the course. The third—what would the third show? Industrious practice? That was boring. She thought for a moment, then added a bit more to the text.

> After that, the club members showed up every day and even began to jump real cakes. Latooth was busy in the kitchen devising perfect confections. Languida was seen with paper and measuring tape muttering about length times width times height. She even tried to measure reluctant club members nose to tail. She began to keep statistics in a little notebook.
>
> Tess, Lady Ponscomb, worked on an article for the *Dibble Gazette*, explaining about the club and its goals. Max could most often be seen organizing the young team members in cat calisthenics and practice races, all to build up their endurance.
>
> Sometimes he forgot himself and ran in tight circles, barking his head off, hysterically happy, herding the cats who would at first stand hissing and arching and fluffing their fur, before eventually losing their collective nerve and, fleeing from their enthusiastic coach, finally jump the course, posting some of their best times, but with disastrous effect on any cakes there.

Gerry snorted with laughter. "I'm not going to fit all that in a three-inch square." She roughed out half a page for the concluding illustration of chapter two and went to bed.

Friday was art history prep day. Gerry felt like a student again, hunched over textbooks making notes. It was a not entirely pleasant feeling. She consoled herself thinking of the salary. She remembered the at least $3,000 she'd need by spring for the cats to visit the vet for just regular checkups. And what if one of them fell really ill or injured themselves, like Graymalkin had?

She also remembered the painting by Paul-Émile Borduas, once hanging incognito on a wall in her aunt's home, and now safely at the auction house in Montreal, awaiting sale. That painting was going to cover the expenses of maintaining a big old house like The Maples and Gerry's nineteen feline wards for years and years. She fretted. What if it was destroyed by fire or stolen? She knew it was insured, but still…

For three hours she applied herself to symbolism in painting in the nineteenth century with little breaks to stretch, prepare coffee or throw wood on the fire. At lunchtime she made a ham and cheese on a croissant, slathering on the mayo and hot mustard. She grated some of the St. Lucian cocoa stick into a little pot of milk, added sugar and vanilla and heated the mixture. Yum. Like very mild hot chocolate. But next time she'd strain it. She reviewed her work schedule. She couldn't believe how fast the days were going by. The end of January already. Okay. Today is art history. Saturday: *Mug the Bug*, two strips. Sunday: hopefully off. Maybe snowshoe or ski if Jean-Louis was around. Monday: more *Mug the Bug*, another two strips. Then she'd be back to having two weeks of advance strips prepared.

*The Cake-Jumping Cats of Dibble* was just for fun, to be squeezed in whenever she could. She figured she must be about half to two-thirds done. Would four chapters be enough? Five? Reluctantly, she returned to the nineteenth century.

At cat feeding and Gerry coffee time she pushed the art history away. There. A week's worth prepared. She stretched and built up the fire. She was just relaxing with her novel and a St. Lucian coffee—plain but good—when the phone rang. "Hello?"

A plaintive male voice asked, "Is this—are you—is this the right number?"

"Uh, for what?"

"For drawing lessons. Can I speak to the instructor?"

"I'm the instructor. Gerry Coneybear."

"Oh." The voice seemed surprised. "Are you an artist?"

Biting back the rude reply she was thinking—no, I'm a gymnast, secret agent, lion tamer—Gerry, regretting the necessity of advertising for new students, patiently replied, "Yes. I'm a successful commercial artist and I graduated in fine arts from the University of Toronto with great honour."

"Oh." There was some hurried whispering at the other end of the line.

Gerry waited, then spoke. "Would you like to come be part of a small group learning how to draw? It's on Wednesdays from one to three and the first class will be this Wednesday."

More whispering. "My wife can't come on Wednesdays," the man said and hung up.

"How peculiar," Gerry mused, and returned to her book.

She'd just got to the part where Charlie the taxman was struggling against the combined charms of Ma's cooking, Pop's whisky and Marriette's good looks, and still fruitlessly trying to get Pop to fill out an income tax form, when the phone rang again.

"Hello?"

"All right," said the same voice as before.

"All right?"

"The class. On Wednesday. Her name's June Conway. She'll be there."

"Oh, good," Gerry replied faintly, wondering how this would play out. "Thank you."

"Thank you!" He hung up.

"Well, whatever next, cats?"

Next involved ordering a pizza. Ten minutes later she remembered Prudence's ready-made dinners in the fridge but it was too late to cancel the pizza. After it arrived, she read lots more of *The Darling Buds of May* sitting in front of the fire, in a hot bath and in bed. She fell asleep dreaming of nightingales singing in a bluebell wood.

Saturday, Gerry worked away at her cartoon strip and took a few calls about the drawing class. One more person agreed to come. Two students made a class so she phoned Judith Parsley, the only one of last autumn's class who'd indicated she would come if winter lessons were offered. Judith was thrilled and signed up.

Gerry buzzed out to Lovering's shopping district and stocked up on staples. She walked from where she'd parked at the grocery store past some of Lovering's smaller merchants. On a whim she went into the British store, which she hadn't yet fully explored.

Too many British candy bars and cookies tempted her. She kept her purchases modest—a Cadbury Flake bar and a package of oat crunchies—though she lingered a long time in front of the Doctor Who mugs. Maybe she'd buy one for her birthday. Hmm. The white one with the iconic red British telephone call box or the blue one with the Dalek saying "Exterminate!"? Too difficult. Perhaps she needed both.

Then she went across the road and had a scone (with everything) and a cup of excellent coffee at the teahouse. Well satisfied with her partial day off, she went home. There was a message on her phone answering machine. "Ah, June says—" whisper, whisper—"June says she's changed her mind." Click.

"Well, really!" Gerry exclaimed and put away her purchases.

Sunday morning she puttered, determined to have a day off. She played with Jay. She picked up a brush and wandered around the house grooming cats, most of whom enjoyed the process. She even managed to coerce the difficult calico cat, Lightning, into letting her gently brush her head and ears. But as soon as she tried to touch the cat's sides or tail, badly scarred from burns received in a previous life, Lightning hissed and scooted away.

Gerry straightened. She put the cat brush on the living room mantel, where it joined a sad-looking poinsettia, a catnip mouse someone's sharp teeth or claws had punctured, and the carved wooden cat Cece and Bea had brought her from their trip to Jamaica.

She was procrastinating. Should she call Jean-Louis or wait for him to call her? The age-old question. She picked up the Jamaican cat and was admiring its smooth curves when the phone rang. "Gerry!" Jean-Louis's voice made her warm. It was nice to be wanted. "I'm so sorry to call so late in the day. I slept in. I was up all night searching for a boy missing on the mountain. We found him this morning."

Gerry, thinking of her art college student, Jerry Pinsky, skiing at Royal Mountain that weekend, asked anxiously, "Is he all right?"

"Yes, yes. Cold but not frostbitten. He knew enough to keep moving. Says he was doing some kind of research, tracking coywolves, measuring the tracks of coyotes and wolves, and their hybrids, but I wouldn't have been surprised if he was running away from home. You should have seen the sour-faced woman who picked him up this morning. I couldn't tell if she was happy to see him or not."

"Oh, I'm sure she was happy," Gerry automatically replied. "Why wouldn't she be?"

"She had a lot of trouble manoeuvring her big Cadillac in the parking lot. I saw her swearing through its windows. The kid just clutched his knapsack and hunched down in the back."

"A blue Cadillac?" Gerry asked. "Kind of old?"

"How'd you know?"

"And a Middle Eastern–looking boy?"

"Yes, but—"

"I've seen her drop the boy and sometimes a couple of girls off at the college. Her husband just died across the road from your place. In the empty house."

"Ah." Silence followed as Jean-Louis digested this information.

"Jean-Louis, how did the boy get on the mountain in the first place? Was he skiing? Had he been one of your students?"

He replied slowly. "No, no, he works part-time in the restaurant on the hill. He must have finished his shift and decided he'd head into the forest for a bit of homework." He yawned. "Gerry, I have to go back to sleep."

"Oh. Okay. I guess I'll just snowshoe."

"Tsst! I was supposed to take you cross-country skiing for the first time! I'm sorry."

"That's okay. We didn't have firm plans and anyway, I forgot to buy boots, I just realized. So we're both disorganized."

"Gerry, would you do me a favour? If I leave the door unlocked, would you take Harriet with you when you go into the woods? Give her a good run?"

Gerry felt pleased that he trusted her with his dog. Over the phone she felt none of that vague discomfort she'd felt in his presence at Cathy's house. And he'd acted appropriately that night when she'd almost run over Harriet. Probably she was getting used to him. "Of course. She's great. It'll be fun."

"I'll leave the leash by the door."

Gerry stuffed a handful of dog treats into her coat pocket and, putting her snowshoes on her shoulder, walked to J-L's house. She cautiously opened the door and stuck her head inside. She was met by the rich sound of full-bodied snoring coming from upstairs and the sight of a big blond husky sitting on the mat, a goofy grin on her face and her tail wagging. Gerry put a finger to her lips. "Shush," she breathed, found the leash and snapped it on.

They headed back onto the main road. Gerry, worried about juggling her snowshoes and a sixty-pound husky against oncoming traffic, tried one of the few dog commands she knew. It had worked when J-L had used it. "Heel?" she said doubtfully, and to her amazement, Harriet, who'd been pulling her along, nose clamped to the ground, came to Gerry's left side and pranced docilely, giving her sly upward smiles, as if to say, "See what a good dog I can be?"

"Good girl! I'll give you a reward when we're off the road." When they were partway up the lane next to Cathy's long front yard, Gerry gave the promised cookie and released the beast.

Harriet covered about 500 yards in what seemed like an instant to Gerry. She panicked. "Harriet!" she cried in a high-pitched voice. The dog responded by galloping back to her side. Gerry gave her another cookie and snapped the leash back on. "We better wait until we're well away from the road. You're too fast!"

At the end of the lane, the uninhabited farmhouse looked forlorn. Snowmobile tracks criss-crossed the open fields around it. Gerry found the trail, put on her snowshoes and let Harriet go. The dog was quickly out of sight but reappeared when Gerry called. Through a combination of intermittently shouting "Harriet!" and rewarding with cookie fragments the grinning, curly-tailed maniac who came bounding back, Gerry figured out how to keep the dog in sight—more or less. They both enjoyed the climb up into the dark pine plantation.

The air was cold and clean and the surroundings silent. Now that she knew what witch's brooms were, Gerry looked at them more closely.

Fantastic clumps made up of short branches growing in all directions, they almost looked like porcupines perched in trees.

One tree's branch hung over the path, and, as Gerry inspected its witch's broom, she saw it had a dark centre. Harriet had rejoined her at that point and sat, nose pointing up at the branch, and Gerry commented, "Harriet, it almost looks like—" She reached up into the tree.

# PART 3

# FISHER

*Graymalkin remembered waking up the night of the attack. The old man had been all right, sleeping. The cat had yawned, showing his fangs, and stretched, each leg thrust out and trembling in turn. When he'd felt refreshed, he groomed for a bit. The old man had turned over, mumbled something and settled. The cat jumped off the bed.*

*The old man had had his bedroom shifted to a room on the main floor of his home. He rarely went upstairs. But that didn't mean the cat couldn't. After a brief snack from the bowl of kibble on the kitchen counter, he'd sprung up the stairs and taken his familiar position.*

*Graymalkin's lookout post, the old man had laughingly described the seat that filled the space in front of a small bow window tucked up high in one of the house's many mismatched gables. Not that the cat cared about architecture. He just wanted to see out. And this window in a spare bedroom was uniquely positioned.*

*Not only could he see his own backyard, snow-covered, stretching through bare trees to the lake, but, to the left, that of the house next door, his former home, which he'd previously shared with a multitude of other cats.*

*Not his style, sharing. He remembered grooming his shoulder complacently. He walked alone. A self-satisfied glint in his eye, he'd contemplated his true name—Defiance.*

*A flutter near the shoreline of the house next door had made him freeze. The hunter's instinct. Sheepishly, he'd relaxed. After all, the flutter couldn't sense him, perched up high behind glass. Perhaps, he'd thought, he should go down there and...*

*The slight motion had repeated. A bird? It had moved from tree to rock to tree. It had to be a bird. He'd hopped off the shelf and made for the way out. The secret way out.*

*From outside, squirrels had worked at a bit of the roof's soffit until it had come away. The cat had made short work of their idea about over-wintering in the old man's attic, dispatching a few of the slower ones. Not that the squirrels had stopped trying, gnawing through drywall not just in the cat's lookout room when he was busy elsewhere.*

*It had been fun to silently creep up the stairs, enter the room, hop from the window seat up onto the tall wardrobe that concealed one of the holes in the drywall and squeeze through into the attic. Fun because he sometimes surprised one or more of the long-tailed rodents. Fun to hear them squeak and scrabble their way towards the exit. And fun to follow them out through the broken bit of soffit onto the ledge where swallows used to nest. Swallows no longer, the cat had thought with satisfaction.*

*He'd jumped from the swallows' ledge to the cherry tree. Its red bark was smoother than he would have chosen in a tree used to descend three stories, but it was the only one within reach.*

*Halfway down, he'd paused, listening. Only the drip of snow melting off the roof. The January thaw made his descent easier. Other times, the cherry tree's bark had been slippery with ice.*

*At the bottom of the tree, he'd paused again and sniffed. A rank odour had assailed his olfactory receptors. Dog. Possibly wild. He'd looked down at the snow in his backyard. No tracks. He leapt.*

*Cold. Wet. He'd repressed a shudder and taken the path to the left toward his former home, hunching a bit. What was in summer a green and secluded aisle between tall fleshy plants with dangling orange flowers had then offered only the shelter of the snowbanks shovelled up by the women as they created a path from their house to the old man's back door. The cat had felt exposed.*

*The chain-link gate had posed no problem. Easy to dig under in the other three seasons, it was likewise easy to kick aside the soggy snow. Nasty stuff, though easier than mud to groom off once one was back inside.*

*In the neighbour's yard, he'd surveyed the house, looking for other cats. Their cat flap (as was his) must be blocked off in winter. Sometimes he saw someone he knew sitting at a window. Not that night. But the flutter.*

*He'd turned his head to the shoreline where small trees gave way to rocks now half-covered in snow. Yes. His head swivelled. There.*

*He'd run along the shovelled path that skirted the back of the house before it turned toward the lake. Sometimes he'd seen the young woman walk down to sit on a rock and gaze at the frozen water. The older woman never went down there. Too smart, he'd thought, to leave the comfort of the house without a good reason. Like investigating a flutter.*

*He'd reached the end of the path and looked up. There. Not a bird. The cat, disgusted, had turned away. A ribbon. A toy for kittens. He'd followed the odour of a strange cat to the house next door, seen the cat drop from a window and proceeded to investigate. His investigations had been insignificant—to him. Back outside, he'd caught another whiff of a rank odour, different from the first, this one more feral.*

*And then it was upon him.*

# 11

Gerry poked the package on the kitchen table with one finger. Black plastic, it gave a bit when she prodded it. "What do you think it is?"

Prudence's eyes became slits. "How should I know?"

Gerry straightened. "I'm going to open it."

"I wouldn't," Prudence advised. "Did you mention finding it to anyone?"

"You're the first. J-L was asleep when I returned Harriet yesterday."

"Well, thank goodness for that," Prudence primly commented.

"Whaddya mean?" Gerry asked, a bit aggressively.

"I mean that the less people who know you took something from the woods, the better. What did you think I meant?"

Gerry, who'd thought that maybe Prudence was referring to any burgeoning romance there might be between herself and J-L, relaxed. "Oh, nothing. I'm going to open it," she repeated a little uncertainly.

"All right. I'm waiting," Prudence said.

Gerry looked at the package. It was a bag about the size Gerry had seen Cathy use to pick up Prince Charles's poop. She giggled insanely. "What if it's dog poo, Prudence? That somebody threw in a tree?"

"Don't be stupid." Prudence sounded cross. "Who would pick up dog poo in the woods? Just get on with it. Here, put these on." She handed Gerry the yellow washing-up gloves from the kitchen counter.

Gerry put them on, squeezed the package and undid the twist tie. She peered in. "It's full of lots of little bags." She dumped them onto the table. The women stared in dismay.

"Oh, shit," Prudence uncharacteristically said. "Put it back right away and call the police."

The police, when they came, were highly suspicious, not of Prudence so much, but of Gerry. How often did she go into the woods? Did she go alone? Who did she meet there? How long had she known J-L? Then the questioning shifted. Had she known Nolan Shrike and forgotten to tell them? Did she know Mrs. Shrike? Did she know any of the students staying at the Shrike house?

It was noon when they left. Prudence and Gerry ate their lunches together. Prudence had made Gerry a ham and cheese during the questioning and munched her own favourite—a peanut butter and sweet pickle sandwich with a bag of potato chips. "Well, I didn't get much housework done this morning," she admitted.

"Don't worry about that. This is serious. Do you think the police think Mr. Shrike was mixed up with drug dealers?"

Prudence shrugged. "Maybe he was in the wrong place at the wrong time. Maybe the dealers used the house next door for meeting and Mr. Shrike came to check the property by chance. That was his job, after all."

"Yee-es. But Mrs. Shrike told me he used to take their dog into the woods for walks. And that's where I found the drugs."

"Did the police tell you what they were?"

"No. A white power, as you saw."

"Could be cocaine," Prudence mused.

"Cocaine? That's so old-fashioned," Gerry said. "And anyway, how would you know? Prudence?"

"How do you think?" her friend replied. "I was a teenager all through the 1960s. You think sex, drugs and rock'n'roll bypassed

Lovering? What I don't know is what drugs people do now. Crack? Pills?"

"Yeah," Gerry said absently. "And grass. Mostly grass that I've seen. But not here," she added hastily. "In Toronto. When I was a student."

"So who does cocaine?" Prudence mused. "It's expensive, right? So. Rich people. But they don't want to traipse up into the woods to buy their drugs. Or into empty houses in the middle of the night. What if the drugs were delivered to them by respectable Nolan Shrike? Or his wife?" She finished her lunch and stood up. "Well, the police seem to have made the connection. We stay well out of it, right, Gerry?"

"Well out," Gerry agreed.

When they met again for a tea around two, Gerry, trying to keep off the topic of drugs, casually asked, "How was Mrs. Smith?"

Prudence put down her teacup sharply. It clanked in the saucer. "Mrs. Smith was fine. But I do not expect, when I'm spending my money, for her to do nothing but talk about you. Your house. The house next door."

"I'm—sorry?" Gerry said, bewildered.

Prudence backed down. "No, I am. I wanted to talk to Mother, tell her about the house being repaired and about my vacation. But all Mrs. Smith kept saying was, 'a child, a child next door,' and when I asked on which side of my house, she said, 'not at your house but at one of the ones you visit—lots of cats.' Well, I knew it must be this place."

At that moment, lots of the cats sauntered into the room so as to be close to the kitchen in case signs of supper preparation began. Gerry knelt down and prepared to light a fire. "No children at Blaise's place and no children in the house next door. What could she have meant?"

Prudence looked at Gerry in exasperation. "Uh, she's a medium, so maybe the spirit of a child?"

"Oh? Oh. A spirit child next door. Meaning a child who died when they were a child? That's kind of sad." She lit a twisted piece of newspaper and applied it to the kindling. "Did she say anything else?"

"That the child was only playing and never meant to hurt anyone." There was a pause. "You haven't felt anything when you've been over there, have you?" Another group of cats entered the room, looking even hungrier than the first.

"Me? Nope. I was looking for a cat. Bob was with me and poked his nose in everywhere; probably got a shock from the Christmas lights in one bedroom. And when I went over with the police, it was all about Nolan Shrike's body, which was not spiritual at all but very real. In a body bag."

"Mrs. Smith didn't mention any of that. But she doesn't get to choose who or what comes through." Prudence appeared to tire of the subject. "Have you enough students coming to your drawing class on Wednesday?"

"How many are enough? Two or three. Judith I can count on. Someone named June Conway can't seem to make up her mind. And another lady—Sharon Wolfe—with an 'e'—the Wolfe not the Sharon. It's just occurred to me, Prudence, by only offering classes during the day on a weekday, I'm making it impossible for working people to attend. Maybe I should do a class on a Saturday morning or something." She looked around her at the assembled cats and grinned. "I swear these guys know when I'm making a fire even if they're upstairs."

"I think while you're teaching two days a week at the college, you should take your weekends off. Re-evaluate in the spring."

Gerry raised her arms, then lowered them and her head. "Yes, oh wise one." She quit fooling and asked, "Are we going to get any more work done here today?"

"I've done the minimum. I'll have a really good clean on Thursday. Do you know what you're going to bake for the drawing class?"

"I thought I'd look through Aunt Maggie's recipe file. Do you want to help me? Look at recipes, I mean, not bake."

Prudence sighed. "No. She and I used to do that. It's too soon. It would only be sad. Maybe someday." She went to finish her chores. Some of the cats, realizing that no supper was yet on offer, dispersed back into the rest of the house. Some, drugged by the warmth of the fire, lingered.

Gerry, welcoming a distraction from drugs and murder and spirit children, opened the drawer in the kitchen table where she knew her aunt's recipes lay. She carried them through to the living room table and plunked herself down.

Aunt Maggie had collected her recipes in a scrapbook. Some were handwritten, some clipped out of magazines or newspapers, and some had been typed. Most pages of the book were stained with brown splotches. Tea? Vanilla?

"Gingerbread Men, Sugar Cookies, Spice Cake," Gerry murmured. "How funny! Cowboy Coffeecake. For cowboys or a cowboy recipe? Marble Butter Cake. Oo, that sounds good." She read the recipe. "Nah, too complicated. But someday." Salivating, she reluctantly turned the page. "Fat rascals! What on earth are fat rascals?" She read the recipe, at the top of which Aunt Maggie had written "Delicious" and "Wow!", then found Prudence vacuuming under the dining room table, an assortment of cats resting on nearby chairs. "Prudence," Gerry said excitedly, "I'm going to make fat rascals!"

Prudence switched off the vacuum and looked at the recipe. She nodded. "You should be able to manage that. Don't overwork the dough. A light hand." She switched the machine back on, then shouted over its noise, "Check if you have enough butter. You can use raisins if you don't have currants." She smiled when Gerry saluted.

Back in the kitchen, Gerry checked her ingredients. Butter and raisins: okay. Annoyingly, she was low on flour. She decided to do a grocery run and, calling to Prudence, "back soon," left.

As she drove past the empty house next door, she noticed first that a path had been shovelled to the front door, and second, that someone had replaced the Christmas wreath. Could Mrs. Shrike be continuing the work her husband had been doing? Who else?

When she returned home, Prudence gave her a message. "A man phoned to say June will be coming to art class on Wednesday." Gerry opened her eyes wide. Prudence continued. "And, Blaise phoned to say Graymalkin is home but should be quiet for a couple of days."

"That's great!" Gerry exclaimed, any exasperation she might have felt at the waffling behaviour of her would-be new art student subsumed in her joy at hearing her neighbour's cat was better.

*Splash!*

Gerry, sedately doing lengths in her lane at the college's pool, hadn't thought diving during the noon free swim was allowed. It wasn't. The miscreant was escorted by a lifeguard out of the pool and pool room. Gerry caught sight of her second cousin David, Doug's youngest son, like her, watching the scene. She beckoned.

He crossed to her lane, flicking his blond hair out of his eyes. Eyes like Doug's: brown, friendly. "Hi, Gerry." They both treaded water.

"Hi, David. It's good to see you. Whatcha been up to?"

"Oh, you know. Christmas holidays I did some skiing." He grinned. "Mostly just played games at home and ate."

She assumed he meant video games. "What kind of games?"

"The ones where you create a world are fun, but I play the exploding head ones with my brothers as well."

"Ew. How's your dad? And your mum?"

A shadow passed over David's face. "Mum isn't doing well. Dad says not to expect much when we visit. She doesn't speak. Doesn't seem to know we're around."

Gerry paused. "I'm sorry. That must be difficult. Is your grandmother involved with you at all?"

"Oh yeah. She likes us to come for a meal. Not Dad. Just the three of us." Gerry's cousin Margaret, the boys' mother, had been recently institutionalized, and, as Gerry knew, there was a good reason for her silence and for her never getting out. But David didn't know any of that. That Margaret's mother, Gerry's Aunt Mary, was even minimally involved with the boys was, in Gerry's opinion, a mixed blessing. But again, David wasn't to know that either, so Gerry just said an innocuous "that's nice," before querying him about school. "How come you're not in my art history class?" she asked.

"Couldn't fit it in. I'm taking three required courses this term: English, French and physical education. Depending on when you sign in, the computer does the scheduling."

"What are your art courses?"

"Painting, printmaking and photography."

"And what's your favourite?"

"Ah, it's between printmaking and photography. I like to do things, make things, rather than paint."

"Like your dad," said Gerry, thinking of Doug's sculpting in neon. "How's the kitten?"

David's face lit up. "She's a terror! She mostly sleeps on my bed. Wakes me up. Wants to play in the middle of the night."

"I know that feeling," Gerry admitted ruefully.

"Hey, you know her brother? The one you gave to the Parsley kids?"

"Yeah. Is he okay?"

"Yeah, yeah, but it turns out it's not the kids the cat likes. It's their dad. It sleeps with him and follows him around. He even lets it into the bar."

"Aw." Gerry envisioned the diminutive kitten Gee attaching itself to the large figure of the recently widowed restaurateur Phil Parsley.

"He calls it Gregory."

"Gregory!?" They laughed. "So everybody who got a kitten changed its name except me. Jay is still Jay."

"Hey, Gerry, I've got a class at one so I've got to go."

"Oh, no! So do I! Race you!" They swam to the shallow end, David won and each darted away to the changing rooms. Gerry wondered, will I ever arrive at this class without being out of breath?

# 12

"While Turner flirted with abstraction—look at *Landscape with a River and Bay in the Background*, making the lyric landscape fuzzy with warm colours—he was essentially Romantic. Artists today still use these techniques.

"Now, in *The Beguiling of Merlin* by Edward Burne-Jones, we find symbolism in full flower. The male and female figures in counterpoise and all around them the sensuous natural world. The tension between the two can be seen at the centre of the canvas where their eyes meet. And there, also at the centre, is the perspective away in the distance. I like the shine of dark fabric and the dull white of skin and flowers. The dreaminess of the artist's treatment was the new thing here."

Gerry paused and took a sip of water as they all stared at the image on the screen. She clicked to von Schwind's *The Knight of Falkenstein's Exploit*. "Germany, even as it became a nation, looked back with nostalgia to a more bucolic time. There were paintings like this one—knights on horses as an ideal." She clicked. "I think even without the title we know what this is about." The painting was Arnold Böcklin's *The Plague*. "Death rides a dragon, dead or dying townspeople lying everywhere. It's kind of rough. Kind of crude. Almost...modern.

"And so to France. To 'les Primatifs,' who thought art should go back to the Greek ideal for symbolism. Symbolism was their goal. It doesn't get more basic than this." Amaury-Duval's *The Birth of Venus* came up in the darkened room, the girl's white body startling in its purity against a blue background.

"So the title makes us think of Botticelli's version. But look how natural Amaury-Duval's Venus is. No shell. No hair from her head coyly covering her private parts. No fabulous attendants. Just a perfect girl standing on the beach, wringing out her wet hair."

She let them admire the painting before continuing. "Another group of painters were the Troubadours. For those who don't know, although you're supposed to have read this section, troubadours were poets and musicians in late medieval times in France and Italy and their theme was courtly love.

"So these artist Troubadours painted small scenes of everyday life that referenced symbols from chivalry. Their faithful rendering of nature was perhaps an indication of things to come. Isn't it fascinating that depending when an artist is born, and where, will influence his or her development profoundly? We artists work away, never knowing if our work will be remembered or sink from view." She paused, reflecting on her own work. Would anyone care about *Mug the Bug* in 100 years?

She snapped back to attention when the sound of a chair being scraped told her someone was restless. "An example of geography influencing artists' content can be seen by considering the city of Lyon in France. From the mid-nineteenth century on, a religious centre, it was where religious symbolism flowered. This resulted in some 'sweet' work such as *The Flight of the Soul* by Janmot, but also in some more powerful work by two artists.

"Pierre Puvis de Chavannes reduced his content to a primitive style that was yet modern. In *The Poor Fisherman*, painted in 1881, the man stands in his boat waiting for something to bite while his wife gathers wild plants from the barren shore.

The absence of colour gives this drab scene some of its power, but it is the central triangle between the man, the woman and their baby sleeping on the ground that draws our eye. We feel how important it is that he catch something.

"The other artist is Gustave Moreau who died in 1898. This painter, like Puvis de Chavannes, was both referencing the past and going forward at the same time. Look at *Helen Before the Scaean Gate,* done around 1880. There's the classical figure, the classical architecture. But look at the brushwork on the red and rusty black bits down here. What energy! That and the wisp of white smoke rising tell us we might be looking at a disaster. A fire? When we investigate the mythology, we find the story involves Helen appearing during a lull in the fighting between the Trojans and Achaeans and acknowledging people from her past, some living, some dead. A moment of great personal sadness." Gerry paused.

The chair scraped the floor again. Gerry looked up sharply. The texting girl was half out of her seat. "And that wraps up symbolism," Gerry said. "We'll get into painting reality on Thursday, and after that, Impressionism. Jerry, could you stay a second?"

Jerry, looking worried, slowly came to the front of the room. "Is it my homework, Miss? I meant to..."

Gerry hastened to relieve his mind. "Didn't get it done? Hand it in on Thursday. I wanted to ask about your weekend."

He looked surprised. "Oh, well, you know. We skied and ate and skied some more. Then, just, ah, partied at the chalet."

"Mm. Sounds like fun. Did you notice—were you aware someone went missing?"

"Yeah, yeah. They were talking about it Sunday when we went to the restaurant for breakfast." He blushed. "More like lunch, actually."

Gerry laughed. "Do you know who was missing?"

"Some guy who worked in the restaurant, I heard."

Gerry felt a bit relieved. At least the foreign boy wouldn't be teased for getting lost on the mountain if and when he returned to college. She didn't know why, but she felt protective of him. "Okay, Jerry. I was just curious."

He left and Gerry slowly packed her bag. Like the kids, she used a knapsack and, as she hoisted it up to one shoulder, she still felt worried about the boy and the two girls in Mrs. Shrike's care. Were they involved with drugs? Was Mrs. Shrike? Why would Mrs. Shrike threaten them? In any case, what could Gerry do?

Gerry twirled the catnip mouse in a circle above Jay's head. The kitten's white paws flashed as she spun in response. At five months, she was three or four times the size she'd been when she arrived with her brothers and sisters last fall. Then they'd been the size of adult mice.

Mother, the most maternal of the cats in Gerry's tribe, had brought the kittens one by one to Gerry's house through the cat flap and onto the dining room carpet. Gerry had nursed them, getting up at night to feed them special cat milk by eyedropper until they could eat solid food. Mother had provided the warmth of her large marmalade-coloured body.

Between them, Mother and Gerry had made a good job of the kittens and four had been adopted into good homes.

Gerry had fallen in love with Jay. She was the most energetic of them all and Gerry loved her white boots and belly and shiny black everything else. Like Bob, Gerry's other favourite, a tuxedo cat, Jay had white whiskers.

These whiskers now twitched as Jay, tired by their game, climbed back into the banana box on the hearth and snuggled into Mother's warmth. The sound of a contented double purring arose from the box.

Gerry leaned over and stroked the adult cat. "Don't worry, Mother, we're keeping little Jay." Mother blinked a couple of times before going to sleep.

Gerry stared at the fire and sipped coffee with a sigh of happiness. This time of day—three, four, four-thirty in the afternoon—was when she almost always paused for breath. What with all her various freelance assignments, and the cats, and shopping for them all, and the daily chores, she sometimes felt that she, like Jay had been, was spinning in circles.

What was really important? Talking about long dead artists and their influences had bothered her. Who was she to evaluate them? They had had rents to pay, children to raise, commitments, chores. Yet they had made fine art while she dabbled with cartoon strips and ideas for children's books.

Her stomach growled. She put a slice of store-bought meat pie in the oven and felt virtuous as she peeled and sliced potatoes, carrots and broccoli. She quietly ate her supper staring out at the frozen lake, at the few lights far away on the opposite shore. Then she changed her clothes and went to get Prudence. She wondered what film they were going to see.

The almost full moon lit her way along the river road. She slowed as she passed the Parsley Inn, gay with lights, its parking lot three-quarters full even this early in the week. She gave a thought to the family there, wondered how Phil Parsley, the owner, was managing without his hard-working wife Betty, how their four kids were coping without their mother.

Gerry sighed. As the car climbed the big hill she looked down to her left. The best view in Lovering, she thought, then checked herself, thinking of several others, including the one from her own backyard.

Across the lake the lights of the little village there, its church and harbour visible, twinkled invitingly. The moon hung off to the right. The sky was a deep dark blue. "I wonder," she mused, thinking what a fine painting it might make.

She was considering the palette she'd select when she saw movement out on the ice. First checking her rear-view mirror, she slowed, then stopped the car, pulling over as much as she could. You never knew in Lovering in winter where exactly the road ended and the snow-filled ditch began. She pushed the hazard lights' button and got out of the Mini. She was halfway up the hill.

She crossed the road and found a place to stand a few feet from its edge. She shivered and folded her arms across her chest, remembering that night she'd watched Doug and others out on the ice, the sickening lurch in her stomach when first one man then another had gone through into the cold lake waters.

But these weren't perpendicular shapes crossing the ice, drawing nearer. These were low to the ground, running.

Gerry straightened. Wolves! Coming from the other side, presumably the forest, to the Lovering side, to hunt in Lovering's forest—where Gerry snowshoed and others skied! Where Harriet went for walks!

She ran to her car, got in and waited. *Night Crossing* she'd call the painting. Her fingers itched for a sketchpad and pencil.

Where she was parked the land fell off abruptly to a long marshy expanse. The wolves had left the ice and reached the first frozen reeds. Of course, they should be easily able to climb to the top, even where the angle of ascent became acute. She thought about wolves, about their smaller cousins, coyotes, and about this new creature—the coywolf.

To her surprise, instead of disappearing as they struggled up the steep incline, the two whatever-they-were veered to her left, found the driveway of a shut-up summer cottage and took that easier, gentler incline up to the road.

They looked neither to right nor left, nor did they appear to take notice of Gerry's car or the road itself. Without hesitation, they crossed and continued along another long driveway that led to a house hidden behind some trees. Boy, those people would get a surprise if they were walking their dog tonight! Or driving out for some reason. Like her. "Oh crap!" She'd caught sight of the car's clock. Ten minutes until the film was supposed to start and she still hadn't picked up Prudence.

"Sorry, sorry," she exclaimed as Prudence for once slid into the passenger seat. "There were wolves and I stopped to watch."

Prudence dismissed the wolves. "Probably coyotes. And it's all right to be late. People like to have a drink first."

"Unusual," Gerry commented. "Booze at a country film show."

Prudence made a face. "Well, it's in a theatre usually used for live productions so I guess the licensing is different."

"What are we seeing anyway?"

"An adaptation of one of Jane Austen's stories, extended and filmed."

"Oh, I love Jane Austen. I read her books when I was a teenager. I should read them again."

"What are you reading now?"

"A set of five novels I found in Aunt Maggie's collection. By H. E. Bates. They start with *The Darling Buds of May*, which I'm almost finished."

"I think that was a television show. When you were little. Maybe the library has DVDs. I'll look next time I'm there."

Gerry pulled into the parking lot for Lovering's grocery store. It was packed with cars.

"You may have to go over to the other side."

"I had no idea showing a film in a little village theatre like this would be so popular." Gerry found a spot and they hurried inside.

People were just leaving the lobby, drinks in hand. Gerry turned to Prudence. "Do you want anything?" Prudence shook her head, so they took their seats. As the lights dimmed, Gerry caught sight of Mrs. Shrike.

The film was pleasant enough. At the interval, people proceeded out of the auditorium, Gerry assumed for more drinks and standing around, chatting. She and Prudence just stood and stretched by their seats. Mrs. Shrike, sitting a few rows below them, sat rigidly in place. People in her row edged around her without speaking.

Odd, thought Gerry. "Oh, Mrs. Shrike," she called impulsively. The woman twisted her neck.

"Oh. It's you." She nodded and turned back to face the stage.

Gerry got up, walked over to Mrs. Shrike and sat down. "How are you?"

Mrs. Shrike kept her gaze forwards. A brown leather purse sat on her brown-skirted lap. "I'm fine," was the brusque reply.

"And how's Sharp? You said he was pining."

"The dog is improving." Did Gerry imagine it, or was there a slight softening in Mrs. Shrike's demeanour?

"I'm glad. I saw him in the car the day you paid me a visit. It's a striking breed. A foxhound, I think you said."

"An English foxhound," Mrs. Shrike replied proudly, turning her head to look at Gerry.

"I heard from my neighbour who works at Royal Mountain that one of your student boarders, er, got lost last weekend. He was working there?"

Mrs. Shrike looked away, her lips tightening. "All my boarders work. At part-time jobs. It's part of how they pay their ways."

Gerry continued in a bland voice. "And the two girls I heard you threatening when you picked them up at the college? Do they have jobs? And why would you say you'd kill them?"

Mrs. Shrike flushed and stood. "I don't have to explain myself to you!" She tried to edge past Gerry. Other moviegoers, returning to their seats, gave them nervous looks. Gerry scrunched her legs to one side to let Mrs. Shrike leave.

"What did you say?" whispered Prudence as the theatre darkened and the film resumed.

"Tell you later," Gerry whispered back.

# 13

"Nooooooo!" wailed Gerry. The kitten Jay, standing on the kitchen counter—no, right on the pan of carefully prepared unbaked fat rascals—leapt off the counter onto the table, to a chair and from there to the floor and out of the room.

"How did you get in here, anyway?" Gerry, who had stepped into the living room to make up the fire, realized she must have failed to properly close the kitchen door. No cats allowed unless they were eating, was the usual kitchen rule.

She surveyed the little teacakes. There was no obvious damage. It must have been the smell of butter that attracted the kitten. There was three quarters of a cup of the stuff to two cups of flour in this recipe. You rolled out the dough and cut it into twenty-four two-inch rounds. Half of them you put on the baking sheet (No need to grease that!), dotted each round with a little blob of butter, and then topped with the other twelve rounds.

"Double-deckers," breathed Gerry, bending low to inspect the biscuits' surfaces. She reached out and picked off a black cat hair, squinted, couldn't see any more, and made her decision. She thrust the pan into the hot oven, set the timer for ten minutes and made a cup of tea. What the eye doesn't see, the heart doesn't grieve, she thought, or the mouth taste.

She was sipping a nice hot Earl Grey when the timer buzzed. She peered nervously at the biscuits and tapped one. She quickly rotated the tray, closed the oven door and set the timer for three additional minutes. The biscuits had risen nicely but the one she'd tapped hadn't had that satisfying hollow feel she'd come to associate with perfectly baked cookies, cakes and muffins.

"And just think," she told herself as she removed the browned biscuits, oozing buttery raisins, and transferred them to a wire rack, "a year ago I couldn't bake a thing!"

She couldn't resist—ate one then and there. After all, there would only be four, including her, for afternoon tea. The fat rascal easily split into its upper and lower halves—flaky, delicious.

She rushed upstairs, washed and dressed, then returned to the living room for a final tidy.

She cleared the table completely and ranged four chairs facing it and the view of the lake out the back window. Then she put a few objects on the table: a stack of old hardcover books, her wooden cat, a jug of dried hydrangeas.

At five to one the doorbell rang. Judith, the one student from last fall's class, left her coat in the hall and followed Gerry into the living room. Gerry explained, "Much warmer in here and close to the kitchen for making tea."

Judith, a tall girl in her early twenties, looked around appreciatively and held her hands out to the fire. "It's a lovely room."

The bell rang again and Gerry let in a woman whose voice she recognized from the phone to be Sharon Wolfe. She took her coat and led her to join Judith.

"Well," Gerry said brightly, "we may be joined by another student. Or not. So tell us, Sharon, what your previous art experience has been."

As Sharon recounted how talented an artist she'd been as a child—"everyone said so"—and how she'd had to "give it up" to raise her children and look after her husband (Here she sniffed deprecatingly.), Gerry allowed her attention to drift. No third car was heard arriving. It was ten past one. She decided to begin.

"Well, I'll try to make sure you get to explore all that potential, Sharon. Let's do a very quick sketch of the objects on the table. We have five minutes."

Judith began and Gerry pretended to begin as she watched Sharon frown and stare at the table. She drew a strong horizontal line to represent the table edge. Gerry leaned forward and said, "Just make quick little strokes with the pencil, Sharon, and try not to think about what you're seeing."

Sharon carefully drew the two legs at the front of the table. Gerry narrowed her eyes and checked the clock. "Time," she said. "Turn the page."

"But I'm not done," protested Sharon.

"These are just preliminary exercises," Gerry explained. "The next one will be longer."

The doorbell rang. "Excuse me. That must be the other student." She went to the front door and opened it. A very short, very fat woman stood to one side, looking at her husband in their car. He in turn was leaning out the window, looking anxiously at her.

"It's all right, Mr. Conway. I've got her." Gerry waved and the obviously relieved man drove off. "Please come in, Mrs. Conway. June."

June Conway stepped sideways over Gerry's door's sill and, still without making eye contact, unzipped her coat. Gerry, trying to fill the social vacuum, found herself chattering. "I'm so glad you could join us. Let me take your coat. Of course we've already begun a few exercises but you'll catch up. Do come this way."

As she seated June in the fourth chair, she saw a look of compassion on Judith's face even as Sharon, when she saw who it was, rolled her eyes up toward the ceiling. Gerry wondered, Is there something I don't know here?

There had already been a few cats by the hearth but now a half-dozen more sidled in and arranged themselves around the room. Bob, the extrovert, hopped up onto the table and posed, sitting blinking at the class. Min Min, all the good places by the fire taken, paused by June's leg, then stretched up and looked at her, one paw tapping her thigh.

"Min Min, I think—" Gerry began, and made as if to remove the old white cat.

But June forestalled her, reached down, scooped up the cat and plunked him on her lap. A vast purring began as June supported the cat and her sketchpad with one hand and grasped her pencil with the other.

"Well, if he's not bothering you," Gerry said.

Gerry made a few suggestions, then went to make tea and pop the scones into a warm oven to reheat. When she returned, all three students were working away. "Tea time," Gerry announced, and put the tray next to Bob. "Help yourselves, please." She poured four cups of tea and they all took a biscuit.

"Mm! Gerry! So good!" said Judith, who was used to this aspect of Gerry's art classes.

"Yes. Er. Very nice. I wasn't expecting tea," said Sharon stiffly. She added, "Thank you."

"Thank you," whispered June, feeding Min Min a buttery crumb.

"They're very rich, aren't they?" said Gerry. "It's the first time I've made them. Have another."

"That's a lovely tray," observed Sharon, examining the portraits of Queen Elizabeth and Prince Philip. "'The Queen's Silver Jubilee 1952–1977,'" she read.

"Is that her wedding anniversary?" young Judith asked.

"Her reign," whispered June, much to their surprise.

"Do you follow the Royal Family?" Gerry asked kindly.

June nodded. "Mugs," she said.

"You collect mugs," Gerry concluded. June nodded again. "Royal mugs?" June nodded vigorously. "Well," Gerry said dubiously, casting about for something else to say, "You would have gotten on well with my Aunt Maggie. She collected ceramics too." She turned to Judith who had found a catnip mouse and was twirling it for Gerry's kitten Jay. "How's Beecham, Judy?"

Judy smiled up at Gerry. "Just like this. Nuts for an hour, then sleeps for half the day. Then nuts again."

"Why'd you call him Beecham?" The five kittens Mother had found and brought home last November had been named by Gerry after letters of the alphabet: Bee, Cee, Dee, Gee and Jay. (They'd actually been named for her first five art students, the first letters of Ben, Christine, Doris, Gladys and Judith herself—but Gerry hadn't told anyone that.) Like the Muxworthys, who had modified Cee to be Cecilia, and the Shaplands who'd called their Dee, Didi, Judith Parsley had made Beecham out of Bee.

"I don't know. It just seemed funny for when he's a crazy kitten and dignified for when he grows up into a serious adult cat. Like Bob." Judith swung the mouse in front of Bob who was still reclining on the table. With one mighty leap, he snagged it out of midair, twisting so he landed on his feet on the hearthrug.

"Some more serious than others!" Gerry exclaimed, and everybody laughed. Bob, now he had the mouse, feigned disinterest and groomed a shoulder. Gerry put her cup down. "Well, I think we should return to drawing, don't you?"

The tea break and cats had done their jobs. The ice was broken. The students seemed looser with their sketching and sad when three o'clock came.

"See you next week! See you!"

As Gerry waved the last one, who happened to be Sharon Wolfe, out the front door, the woman leaned close and whispered, "She's a hoarder," and jerked her head in the direction of June Conway's disappearing car.

Gerry, thinking of her Aunt Maggie's collection of cats, now in her care, and of ceramics, now cherished by Andrew, simply said quietly, "Nobody's perfect," and shut the door.

She went to tidy away the cups and leftover biscuits. "Just the thing for Prudence to have with her tea tomorrow," she told the cats, most of whom were milling in anticipation of their supper.

By the time she saw to their needs and did a few chores, it was time to think about her own supper. She gazed at the interior of the fridge, uninspired. I wonder what Cathy's doing? she thought and phoned her. As she walked over to Cathy's, fifteen dollars to pay for her meal tucked in a mitten, she felt a soft breeze on her cheeks and noticed the stars were invisible. "Snow coming," she murmured and let herself into her friend's house.

What with sleeping in after a fun night at Cathy's—eating a scrumptious meat loaf with tomato sauce, baked potatoes with sour cream and broccoli in cheese sauce, followed by apple crisp and ice cream in front of the TV—being late picking up Prudence, and rushing to prepare for her art history class, it was a frazzled Gerry who dashed from her car across the circular driveway at the college's main entrance.

Someone else must have been running late, as the midnight-blue Cadillac screeched up, disgorged its load of foreign students and screeched away. Gerry caught a glimpse of Mrs. Shrike's angry face, but only a glimpse. The students scattered like frightened mice. Gerry spotted the one she wanted and stepped in front of him. "Hello. Remember me?" He obviously didn't. "We went on the tour at the beginning of term. You thought it was spring and I explained—"

"Yes, yes. What do you want?"

She took a deep breath. "I'm a teacher here." His attitude changed. He assumed a look of respect. She felt absurdly gratified. "I teach art history and—" His face lost interest. She continued, "And I just wanted to say, if you need advice, or even a place to stay, please contact me. I'm Gerry Coneybear and I know about last weekend, how you got lost on the mountain." His jaw slackened and his eyebrows rose. "And I know the woman you live with is a bit difficult, so—"

"With respect, you don't know anything. I didn't get lost." He straightened, trying to look dignified. "I was conducting research. Now, excuse me, I have class." He walked away.

She felt foolish and awkward. That told me, she thought.

"Well, obviously, artists had been depicting reality all along, so what do we think was new at this time?"

Silence.

Gerry sighed. Either no one had bothered to do the reading or they just didn't care. She let her glance stray outside where a sky of such dullness made her feel equally dull. She plowed on. "In the late eighteenth and early nineteenth centuries, remarkable progress was made in landscapes and portraits. With the former—" Gerry clicked through a few images. "—we have, for the first time, artists travelling much further than before for their scenes—the Americas, both North and South, and the Middle East were new locales.

"But what about the artists who stayed in Europe? Well, many German artists like Caspar David Friedrich in his *The Sea of Ice* painted or presented in 1824, rejected the Italian ideal countryside in favour of more harsh subjects. Look at the jagged shards of ice—broken, overlapping—and the dull sky. Pretty bleak. Can be seen out my living room window." Some of the students laughed. Gerry clicked to the next image.

"A French painter named Camille Corot managed to combine realism with lyricism. Look at *Peasants under the Trees at Dawn* painted mid-nineteenth century. Look how loose the technique is. Everything is just as the watcher would have seen it: the light slanting from an open to a wooded area; the workers' bodies just shape and colour; the tree spreading over the scene. It's very humble really. Look at that goose standing to one side." She paused.

"Now we come to the Barbizon school, so named for a village south of Paris where artists would go to find the countryside. Jean-François Millet also painted peasants performing tasks. He was much admired for his truthfulness.

"Another 'realist' who gets mixed reviews from art historians is Gustave Courbet. Look at *Bonjour Monsieur Courbet*, in which the artist is the central figure. I feel his choice to paint the three humans with such crisp clarity makes them appear 'laid over' the smudgy, rougher brushwork he used for the landscape behind them. Even the dog looks posed. But Courbet was popular in his lifetime and many painters emulated him." Gerry presented another image.

"If you can't see what I mean, compare the Courbet with this one and the one after this. First Leibl's *Three Women in Church*, in which the colours of the women's dresses are only slightly different from those in the background. They are women at worship but they are also shapes beautifully tied into and contrasting with their surroundings. I like this painting very much. It is simple but that simplicity has been achieved through Leibl's superlative technique. As is the case with the next."

Click. She heard sighs from the back of the room. "Last one. Rosa Bonheur was much admired for her depiction of animals, working animals such as these oxen in *Plowing in Nivernais,* exhibited mid-century.

"So that's an overview of realism in the nineteenth century. Any questions?" There weren't any. "I think we'll hear your thoughts on the topic next Tuesday, and Thursday as well, if necessary. If you haven't yet read this section of the textbook, please read it this weekend and I think, instead of comparing and contrasting paintings from that period, for homework I'd like you to write two pages minimum on the historical context in which realist painters found themselves. In other words, prove or disprove that their art was a product of its time. Thank you. Have a nice weekend."

As they shuffled from the room, Gerry glanced out the windows along one side. Thick heavy snowflakes were dropping slowly out of the sky. She groaned. She foresaw a slow drive home. Again.

She drove carefully and found Prudence waiting with her coat on. Gerry slid into the passenger seat. “Good practice for winter driving. No sudden movements and you should be fine.”

Prudence got behind the wheel. “Good fat rascals, by the way. I ate both of them.”

“Thank you. You were meant to. How’s everything?”

To her surprise, Prudence sighed. “It’s the February blues, I guess. And I just got back from vacation! How come the shortest month seems the longest?”

Gerry replied, “And it’s leap year, so it’s got twenty-nine days instead of twenty-eight.”

Prudence changed the subject. “I walked over to Blaise’s today at lunch. Saw the cat. He’s walking around, stiffly. Great big scar on his side. The fur was shaven off, of course. Looks terrible.”

“I’ll go over tomorrow,” Gerry decided.

“Oh. And your friend phoned. J-L, he called himself.”

“And?”

“Said he’s got to work tomorrow in the day but has the evening off and would you like to go for a moonlight ski? Very romantic.”

“It won’t be when I’m slipping and sliding all over the woods. It’ll be my first time, remember?”

“Really?” Prudence asked, putting extra incredulity into her voice.

Gerry lightly tapped her knee. “Miss Smartypants. My first time cross-country skiing. Anyway, if this snow keeps up there won’t be a moon to ski by.”

They arrived in Prudence’s driveway uneventfully. “That was really good, Prudence. I didn’t have to correct anything. You can drive!” A pleased-looking Prudence waved goodbye and let herself into her house.

As Gerry drove home, she enjoyed the rhythm of the falling flakes of snow, lit up by her car headlights, coming at the windscreen, and, for some reason, thought of the fireflies that flashed among the trees and above the lawn at The Maples in summer. Could they be the subject of a backyard painting? When did fireflies get born, anyway? May? June?

She slowed as she drove down the big hill. The village across the lake was less visible but even more magical through the falling snow. Of the four-legged hunters of a few nights ago, there was not a trace.

# 14

Gerry heated a can of ravioli and buttered two slices of crusty bread. She settled at the living room table with a sigh of pure joy. Outside it was still snowing, but she was safe in her cozy home, and her work—that is to say, the part that was regimented by others—was over. She pulled her various project piles closer and drew up a work schedule for her freelance work.

Number one would always be *Mug the Bug*. She'd need to do five episodes over the weekend. "One tonight," she murmured, "and one each day until Monday. I'll do them with my morning coffee. Then I'll know they're done." She scrunched the loose skin on the back of Bob's neck. As usual, he ornamented the table. Little Jay, after zipping around the house like a crazy thing for an hour, had suddenly conked out on Gerry's lap.

"What if Mug met a kitten like Jay, Bob?" Bob blinked wisely. "Hm, I suppose you're right," Gerry concluded, remembering what Jay had done to a luckless spider that had been inhabiting a dark corner. "Still, Mug might be too small for the kitten to eat. What else, what else?" She looked outside. "A talking snowflake? Haven't I already used that?" She noted it anyway. "Oh my gosh, I have to get going on the greeting cards. What's the next holiday? Besides my birthday, of course."

She wrote down under cards: Mother's Day and Father's Day and felt her throat ache at the thought of her parents buried just a few hundred yards away in the little graveyard of St. Anne's Church. "In the cold, cold ground," she muttered; then, feeling the heat of the kitten on her lap, told herself firmly, "They'd want me to enjoy my life, not feel sad."

She fooled around with a few ideas for Mug giving cards to his parents. Okay, she thought, one Mug strip tomorrow and then the rest of the day on greeting cards. I should just make this a *Mug the Bug* weekend.

She was already caught up for the art history class for the following week. "What am I going to bake for the drawing class next Wednesday?" she asked Bob. He stretched on his side, his four legs trembling with pleasure, then curled and dozed. "You're no help," she complained. She cuddled Jay to her chest, got up and retrieved her aunt's recipe scrapbook.

Jay, miffed at being woken, jumped down and toddled off to find Mother. Once Gerry was reseated, Min Min petitioned for her lap. She lifted him up. "Hello, my old friend. How are you?" Min Min started up his motorboat while Gerry selected her next baking project.

She read the directions carefully. Very specific. She could do that. What was it Prudence said? Light hands with pastry, strong hands with bread. Not that she'd ever made bread. She set the recipe aside. Okay, now what?

She had no private commissions pending, which was a bit worrying. She decided to run an ad. But was February the right month to run it in? Better ask Judith, who worked at the paper. She made a note on her calendar. What else?

The view across the lake popped into her mind. The idea of creating fine art, almost from the moment she'd moved into The Maples, had been bothering her. Art for art's sake, without any financial motive. Teaching the art history class had reinforced this craving.

Make a list, her practical brain suggested. 1. Check your supplies. 2. Take photos of the scene. You're not going to set up an easel by the side of the road in winter.

Depositing Min Min on the table, she prepared her camera and looked through her sadly depleted collection of watercolours, acrylics and oils. Hah. She felt a visit to Montreal coming on. Which reminded her: when was that art auction, anyway? She yawned. If she made a coffee now, she'd be up all night. She made a tea instead and sketched, introducing a wary *Mug the Bug* to a curious Jay the kitten.

Friday morning, she phoned Blaise, told him she'd bring lunch, and made two ham and Swiss on croissants. Then she worked until noon and headed over to visit Blaise and Graymalkin. Her friend had left his front door open and called out as she let herself in. "We're in the kitchen." She went through.

There they were: the cat on the old man's lap in the reclining chair in the kitchen. Gerry kissed Blaise and set out their lunch. She looked at Graymalkin. Last time she'd seen him had been at the vet's more than two weeks ago, when he'd been near death. Now, except for the absence of fur on his left side and the incision, which ran from his spine and disappeared under his belly, he looked as usual.

"Hello, Gray," she said softly and let him sniff her fingers. He licked them. "Ham and cheese," she laughed. "I packed a little container for him if he's allowed."

"Of course he's allowed." Blaise gestured expansively. "Here today and gone tomorrow. Let him have it." The cat jumped carefully onto the floor near the little container of food.

"It must still hurt," Gerry commented, handing Blaise his sandwich.

"It's good it's winter," Blaise agreed. "He doesn't want to go out so much. I had Cathy close the door of the bedroom with the hole in the ceiling. Have to get that fixed before the squirrels start coming into the house."

"And the hole in the attic. I bet the cat was keeping them out of there. Tea?"

Blaise nodded, so Gerry put the kettle on. They chatted about this and that and when she saw he was tiring, she left.

She went home, got her wallet and car keys and her camera, and drove to the nearest sporting goods store, where she purchased a pair of cross-country ski boots. As she drove back along the river road towards Lovering, she decided today was the day she'd cross the ice bridge.

When she got to the ferry landing, she turned, paid the man sheltering in the trailer there and drove onto the ice. The road had been plowed and was marked with old Christmas trees, stuck in the snowdrifts either side. The sun had come out so she got out her camera and stopped halfway to take some beautiful shots up and down the river. Then she continued across to the little town where she remembered getting french fries so many times with her parents, but in the summer, when they could cross the river by ferry. Drenched in vinegar and salted, the fries were as good as she remembered. I should do this more often, she said to herself as she drove back to the Lovering side. And wasn't there supposed to be an awesome gourmet food store near the monastery where the stinky cheese came from? A summer outing by ferry, she promised herself.

When she passed the viewpoint for her proposed wolf painting, she stopped again and took a few photos, returning home where she produced not one but two Mother's Day cards.

"I'm on a roll, cats," she congratulated herself as she fed them their suppers and made herself a coffee. It was a new flavour: Belgian chocolate. She smacked her lips. "Just what I wanted." She ate some cookies and nuts and went back to work.

She had sketched Mug, an almost invisible speck on the page, handing his equally tiny mother a huge pompom of a flower and was pondering the text for the card when the phone rang. "I've got pizza," the male voice at the other end of the line stated.

"I'll be right over," Gerry replied. Grabbing her new boots and the rest of her ski equipment as best she could, she arrived at Jean-Louis's door in a confusion of skies, poles, and leaping husky.

J-L laughed. "Just leave the equipment outside. I'll show you how to bundle them for carrying later. Right now, we have hot pizza." He'd ordered the meat lovers' and it smelled wonderful. "Fuel for the skiing," he said through a greasy mouthful. "Beer?"

Gerry, trying not to feed all her pizza to Harriet, swallowed and wiped her mouth. She shook her head. "Not a fan. Too yeasty." He handed her a can of pop. "How are things on the mountain? Did you happen to hear if that boy ran away?"

J-L looked at her for a moment. "Ah yes, you know him. Well, according to him, he hadn't run away. According to him, he was doing wildlife research. A teacher confirmed it." He took a swig from his beer.

Harriet rested her head on Gerry's knees and she felt drool seep through her pants' leg. "Research. Yes. So he told me. Wait a minute. You talked to his teacher?"

J-L gave her a blank stare. "No. Of course not. Someone in management at the mountain told me."

Remembering the bag of drugs she'd found in her local woods, Gerry was suddenly appalled at the idea that the boy might somehow be mixed up in drug dealing.

"What? What did you just think of?" J-L asked curiously.

"Oh, well, I don't think I told you, but I found drugs up in the woods." His expression didn't change. "In a bag in a tree." She sipped her ginger ale. She finished rather lamely. "I'm worried about the boy. That's all."

"I heard about that," he said slowly. "About the drugs."

"How?"

"Prudence must have told me when I phoned and left the message."

Gerry wiped her mouth, thinking, it's not like Prudence to blab.

J-L snapped at the dog. "Harriet, that's enough. Sit! Gerry, you shouldn't feed her. She'll beg all the time. Anyway, turns out the boy, who's from Iran, by the way, is supposed to be learning engineering but has also been studying environmental science. So he *was* on the mountain looking for wolf, coyote or coywolf tracks." He shrugged. "That's his story." He mused, "The coywolf: neither one thing nor the other."

"You told me before. But you don't believe him?"

"You want to split the last slice?" Gerry nodded. "You know, the truth is a funny thing. People tell part of it and feel virtuous enough to make you believe them."

"You're pretty suspicious."

"Not of you, Gerry."

She blushed, trying to think if she'd told any partial truths lately. She decided she hadn't. She raised her last pizza crust and looked at J-L. He grinned and nodded. She threw it at Harriet, who'd been sitting nicely since J-L had so ordered her and smiled at J-L. "What you see is what you get. We ski?"

After they got the boots on and the unfamiliar feel of their hard soles had enticed Gerry to try an impromptu tap dance on the cottage's hard wood floor that had entertained at least Harriet, they went outside. "I have a trail out the back here. No need to go on the road."

The ski boots fit easily into the bindings and the poles were grasped just the way you'd expect. Gerry was poised expectantly when J-L said, "Wait, wait. Do you have any wax?"

Gerry's baffled look was his response. He took off his skis and, telling her to do the same, went back into the house.

Gerry crouched, fumbling with the bindings. What had been easy to step into was harder to undo especially when an affectionate dog was licking your face and inviting you to play. J-L came outside to find Gerry, skis still attached, rolling on the ground laughing as Harriet alternately pounced and retreated. "Oh my God. Children, children, time to ski. You know what? Just stay there." He knelt in the snow and took a small tube out of his pocket.

"What's that?" Gerry laughed. "Industrial-sized lip-balm?"

"This, *mademoiselle*, is ski wax, for those so old-fashioned as to still be using wooden skis. Lucky I have some. You get all sorts on the mountain." He brushed snow off the bottoms of Gerry's skis and rolled wax on. Then he hauled her to her feet. Then he hugged her. "*Petite peste*," Gerry thought she heard him mutter.

As they stood, ready to go, the full moon came out from behind a cloud. The night was still and quiet except for the odd car going by behind them and the distant sound of a snowmobile up in the woods. "Remember one thing," he said. "If you can skate, you can cross-country ski. Can you skate?"

"Actually, yes, I can, rather well in fact," said Gerry, as she took a tentative step.

"So don't step. Slide, as if you were on ice. I'll go first." He quickly swooshed through the fresh fluffy snow and passed through an opening in a stone wall into the open field beyond. She realized that the track they were taking must have been made by the snowmobile parked at the side of his house. Packed down, then covered in a few inches of fluffy snow, the trail the machine had made was really good.

Gerry followed slowly and when she got to the wall, shuffled through the gap. J-L quickly skied across the field and Gerry tried to copy his arm motions. She fell down. He returned. "Don't worry about the arms. Get the legs right first. I'll go next to you for a bit so you can see." He held the poles tucked under his arms and propelled himself forward using just leg power. "See?" he called from the end of the field. "Like skating."

She gamely tried the same trick but over she went again. Harriet, who thought it was all a game, bounded over and pounced on Gerry's chest. "Oof! Get off, dog!" Gerry scrabbled a bit before she figured how to stand up with long sticks strapped to her feet. She waved. "Okay, I'm coming." This time, using the poles for balance, she crossed the field successfully.

"You're doing well," J-L encouraged. "Let's go on."

And so, by fits and starts, they crossed field after field until they came to the familiar farmhouse that signalled to Gerry they were joining her usual path into the woods.

As they crossed the train tracks, they saw the red rear lights of a snowmobile way off in the distance, heading alongside the tracks to Lovering. "They park behind the bar, have a few beers, then go out on the trails again," J-L told her. "We'll have to be careful."

Gerry, having struggled sideways up the little slope to the tracks after J-L had simply run up it, hardly heard him. She was looking in some trepidation at the little slope on the other side of the tracks—her first downhill.

J-L skied down it, stopped and turned. "Just keep the skis straight, about a foot apart, bend your knees, lean forward and let gravity do the rest."

Gerry followed his instructions. And all might have gone well. However, neither of them had allowed for Harriet, who chose the moment when gravity propelled Gerry downhill to dash in front of her. Gerry swerved and fell into the very deep, snow-filled ditch to the side of the path.

"Are you all right?" said a laughing J-L who'd dropped his poles to pull her out. She was covered in snow.

"Yes. I suppose. Is Harriet all right?" asked Gerry. She spat snow out of her mouth. "Yes. I see she is." The dog was pursuing whatever scent had caused the incident. Gerry, acutely aware of J-L's hands brushing snow off her body, shivered.

"Are you cold? Do you want to go back?"

"No, no. I want to go up into the woods. It's so beautiful."

Organized again, they entered the old forest.

Giant oak, maple and hemlock supported the starry, moonlit sky. They stayed on the snowmobile trail and passed the sugar shack. Now a long winding ascent began. Gerry, who had to do it all sideways, was in a sweat by the time they reached the top. They paused and J-L produced two flasks from his backpack. He held up one. "Water." And then the other. "Whisky."

Gerry made a face. "Water, please."

He smiled as he handed her the one flask and sipped from the other. "That worked out. Want some chocolate?"

Gerry's happy expression made him laugh. "A little positive reinforcement for all your hard labour. No, I haven't forgotten you." From his pocket he took out a large dog cookie and gave it to Harriet. "Keep going?"

"Maybe for a bit," Gerry said.

They entered the darkest part of the woods—the plantation of pine Gerry's Uncle Geoff had planted many years ago. In amongst the tight rows of trees, the path narrowed. The temperature dropped and the moon's light dimmed.

The land dipped as they left the pines, moving back into the mixed deciduous forest, and Gerry successfully coasted down, keeping a careful eye out for Harriet. Bisecting the path was a small creek where tall reeds were frozen in ice. Gerry came to a halt and looked to either side, wondering where the dog was. Jean-Louis had gotten farther ahead of her and she couldn't see him either. Off to one side, where the reeds ended and willow shrubs began, she caught a glimpse of the tip of a ski. "J-L?" she called uncertainly. "Harriet?" she called, and was reassured to hear the dog crashing through the underbrush.

Gerry edged off the path, stepping, not gliding, on the creek's fragile surface. Little air pockets trapped under the ice collapsed under her skis. Brittle reeds shattered. When she was a yard from the ski tip she reached out with one of her poles, parting the willows.

She jerked back in surprise, slipped and lurched forward, fell, landing painfully on one elbow. She looked up at the figure slumped on the snowmobile, still wearing its tinted helmet, blood dark at its throat.

# PART 4

# COYWOLF

*Defiance tentatively stretched. His wound pulled but he didn't feel any pain. It felt good to arch and bow, extend his back legs one at a time, then retract them. He sat and groomed for a bit, then stared out the sliding back doors of his kitchen. The old man was asleep in his chair where the girl had left him.*

*Defiance had to admit, she was growing on him. The ham and cheese had been a nice touch. He dimly remembered her soft hands holding him together when he'd been slipping between pain and endless sleep; the warmth of her chest as a terrible coldness began to overtake his body.*

*Then, nothing for a time until he woke to sickness in a cage. He'd thought he was back with the pet adoption agency; that the old man had given him up. But soon he became aware of the old man's voice speaking softly, telling him he had to get better and come home again.*

*That had encouraged him enough that he concentrated on recovering, eating and drinking when permitted, submitting to the many different sets of hands that seemed to mean well, though they sometimes caused him pain.*

*And now he was home.*

*It was a sunny afternoon and chickadees hopped and chirped in the shrubbery. His whiskers twitched. Just wait, birds, he thought, just wait until spring. His head jerked as one bird flew close to the glass, pulling up at the last moment.*

*It was no good. He couldn't get out. In resignation he composed himself on the mat, put his front paws together and let his mind drift.*

*A fishbowl for a hat. A child without a scent. Coloured lights. A ribbon fluttering in a tree. A black and white cat falling, falling.*

*He opened his eyes. That part had been real. He remembered the sound the cat's body made when it hit the snow under the window. Whump! Fine particles had risen into the air. The cat had stood up, shaken itself, seen him and taken off around the corner of the vacant house.*

*He'd raced after it, and both of them had been surprised to see the goldfish bowl followed by the rest of the man in a one-piece suit exit the house through a window.*

*But hadn't goldfish bowl already driven away on its noisy machine? Maybe there were more than one of them. Goldfish bowl had sauntered down the road after leaning a piece of wood against the window.*

*The black and white cat had leapt up onto the window ledge and slithered behind the plywood into the house.*

*Defiance hadn't even considered. He'd followed.*

*Broken glass gave him some difficulty in his landing. He cursed as he tiptoed between the pieces. He sniffed for scent of the other cat.*

*The interior of the house smelt strongly of mice. Distracting. Then he caught a trace of the cat. Female. Scared. She would hardly be likely to return to the upstairs room where the weird odourless child lived. He prowled the rooms on the main floor.*

*The scent. Stronger. This way.*

*Another scent overlay that of the female. He'd followed it to the back of the house where his nose also told him this had been the food room.*

*The black and white cat was sniffing a body lying on its side. Blood oozed from under the man's chin. Defiance had recognized the look in the eyes: the glazing over when life is just leaving.*

*The other cat sensed his presence and puffed her fur defensively. Even so, he had seen how painfully thin she was. Suddenly, beating on her hadn't seemed so much fun. He allowed her to pass.*

*He was alone with the body. Just meat now. Not his kill. He yawned.*

*He jumped up onto the long shelf that followed the row of windows along the lake side of the room. On the snow outside he could see the reflection of flickering Christmas lights from above. He heard a child first laugh then sob.*

*He blinked and woke, glad not to relive leaving the dead body, going outside, and the horrible attack he'd just barely survived. Back on the nice safe mat at the back door of his nice safe kitchen. Behind him the old man gently snored. Outside, little snowflakes began to fall.*

# 15

Gerry sifted the flour and salt into the mixing bowl. She measured the shortening and cut it into the flour, first with a knife and fork to break it into manageable chunks, and then with the pastry blender.

The pastry blender was old: five pieces of wire curved and embedded in a worn wooden handle, contoured to fit her closed palm. She pressed and scooped until the mixture resembled breadcrumbs.

She paused and stared out the kitchen window where a storm raged. Wind gusts off the lake blew snow that piled up around her car. The sky was grey.

She consulted the recipe dreamily. She should have made the pastry for the Eccles cakes yesterday. It was supposed to chill overnight. Oh well. A few hours this morning would have to do.

She mixed lemon juice, egg and water in a teacup and added it to the large bowl of crumbs. Using first a fork and then her hands, she formed a smooth ball of dough.

She heard Prudence's voice in her head. "Light hands. Light hands make light pastry; heavy hands make edible rocks," but even that didn't make her smile.

She rolled the dough out, folded it and repeated. Then she wrapped it in waxed paper and put it into the fridge.

Still in a dream, she took her coffee and wafted into the living room. Cats strolled by on private business; Jay and Ronald played by the fire; Bob, Min Min and Mother looked on indulgently.

Min Min, as he'd been doing lately, asked for her lap. It was given him. I'm relaxing as the dough chills, Gerry thought. Sounds like a soap opera on *The Muppet Show*. "As the Dough Chills." Cue melodramatic music and Miss Piggy, she thought.

She was beginning to feel better. Home, cats and routine were replacing the nastiness of the last few days.

She remembered the dead body on the snowmobile, her shrill cry for help. She supposed Jean-Louis must have had a cellphone and used it because suddenly help had been there—police officers arriving on snowmobiles and floundering through the snow.

She didn't really remember the ski back to J-L's, just the questions there and that her teeth were chattering when she was given a mug of hot tea with whisky in it.

She remembered falling asleep on the couch and someone covering her in a fuzzy blanket. She smiled as she remembered extending her feet only to encounter at the other end of the couch a large tightly compressed furry friend—Harriet, also succumbing to slumber. How comforting her warmth had felt. As had the warmth from the cottage's wood stove.

She remembered passing between sleep and wakefulness, overhearing bits of conversation between J-L and, she supposed, a police officer. J-L's voice was a low rumble, the other voice was clear.

"What were you thinking of, taking her up there?" Mumble, mumble. "Are you kidding me?"

Then she thought someone else arrived, much later, and had another conversation, this time completely inaudible, with J-L.

It was eight o'clock Saturday morning when he walked her home and she fed her cats before falling into her own most welcome bed.

She'd slept all day, then woken to find Bob staring down at her hungrily. She thought she had a sore throat but was distracted by phone calls from, first, J-L and then the police.

Later, as she'd been sipping tea and staring at *The Cake-Jumping Cats of Dibble*, trying to plot the next chapter (Would Queen Atholfass find love with the ace cake-jumper Crazy Legs Cucina from the next village? Or would a new character arrive, a dachshund named, say, Barkey Barkington—Barky Barkison? A rival for Lady Ponscomb's paw; a dog even more annoying than Max, Count Scarfnhatznmitz?), she realized her throat did hurt.

Gloomily, she'd stared out at the dark backyard, cleaned the cat boxes and gone up to bed. She woke sweating several times Saturday night and dreamt not of the two recent murders but of her mother. Oddly, part of her feverish brain noted.

Her mother carried the infant Gerry at her side in a green sling while the adult Gerry watched and was simultaneously in the sling.

Her mother put the sling down on the floor and when the adult Gerry picked it up, it contained a cat, a new cat, not one of her own. She put the sling over her neck and followed her mother, who was walking outside now, in the streets of Riverdale, the Toronto neighbourhood where Gerry grew up.

They were on a garden tour. Her mother would walk up to a house, go to its gate and enter the garden, admire the flowers, caressing them, then exit and repeat the process at the next house.

Meanwhile, Gerry and the cat followed her meekly, until at one house Gerry felt the cat struggling to climb out of the sling. Terrified it might escape and be lost or run over by a car, she called to her mother. As her mother turned, feverish Gerry woke up.

Except for struggling downstairs to do cat chores, she'd spent Sunday in bed, trying to read the second book in The Darling Buds of May series: *A Breath of French Air*. The Larkin family, depressed by a long rainy English summer, crossed to France for what they hoped would be sun and fun. But the weather was as bad on the

French coast as in England and they had to amuse themselves without swimming and tanning. Instead they indulged in flirting, subsequent jealousy and copious amounts of alcohol.

Gerry could only read for short periods before falling asleep. The winds of France died down and the Larkin family got their sunny vacation. She finished the book.

Monday she'd been able to get up and shuffle around as Prudence, who'd cadged a ride from her neighbour Charlie, vacuumed and made cups of tea and a batch of chicken soup. She'd brought DVDs of the television show of *The Darling Buds of May* and Gerry snuggled up on the lumpy old couch in the living room, several cats keeping her company, watching and getting to know the Larkins through the interpretations of excellent actors and actresses.

By Tuesday morning Gerry had been in the sniffling stage of the cold. It was a good thing the art history students were to present their homework, as she was only barely able to sit with a pile of tissues and intermittently blow.

With relief she'd reached the end of the class. A few kids still hadn't presented so she said, "We'll finish painting reality on Thursday and I'll give a brief introduction to Impressionism, and your homework assignment for the weekend."

She'd made it home and into bed.

Today she'd woken feeling much better. The stuffy head was gone; she just had a little cough. So, after washing her face and hands well (She didn't want to infect her students!) she'd made the dough for her Eccles cakes.

On the back of the handwritten recipe, Aunt Maggie had noted some facts about the origin of Eccles cakes. Gerry read them as she drank her coffee.

The cakes were at least 300 years old and were said to celebrate the founding of the church in Eccles, a town near Manchester in central England. Apparently Eccles, the town, derived its name from the ancient Greek for church. Gerry thought of the word ecclesiastic (which she had a fuzzy impression meant something to do with religion) and the penny dropped. The church building in Eccles was almost 1,000 years old, so Eccles cakes had probably been served at fairs in Eccles since before people wrote recipes down.

She sighed and patted Min Min and thought about the Shrikes, the drugs, snowmobilers—alive and dead—and the house next door. And Jean-Louis. Something about how the police had treated him hadn't been the same as the way they'd treated her.

She went into the kitchen and took the dough out of the fridge. It was hard. "And I'm supposed to roll this?" she said doubtfully. While she was waiting for the dough to soften, she made the next part of the recipe: the filling. "Combine butter, brown sugar, currants and cinnamon." She tasted a bit. "Mm. I could just eat this."

She rummaged in the back of the recipe drawer where Prudence had told her cookie cutters were kept. She needed a three- to four-inch round one. She found it among the hearts and snowflakes, the Santa Clauses and pumpkins, and she found something else—a child's plain, old, exercise book.

"What's this? More recipes?" Taking another mouthful of the lovely buttery, sugary currant filling, she went back to her rocking chair and opened the book.

Not recipes. Her Aunt Maggie's name written on the cover, the heading: Tales of Lovering, True and Imagined.

She smiled when she saw the date. April 17, 1958. Aunt Maggie had been ten years old and she'd been writing stories. "The Talking Dog," "The Laughing Child," "The Singing Milkman."

"Oh, these are so cute!" she exclaimed, then saw what time it was and rushed back into the kitchen.

She scattered flour on the counter and the rolling pin and rolled the dough out thinly, making as many rounds as she could with the cookie cutter. She put a teaspoon of the filling in the centre of each round and drew the edges together until she had a few dozen little parcels.

More flour was strewn and each parcel flipped and carefully rolled out again, but not as thinly. Gerry preheated the oven and placed the cakes on the baking trays, brushed each with beaten egg, sprinkled them with sugar and scored three times crossways with a sharp knife.

"More fiddly than I thought," she muttered as she popped them into the oven and dashed upstairs for a wash and change of clothes.

A lovely smell greeted her return. She removed the now golden brown cakes and prepared the tea things for later. The doorbell rang. Well, at least one student had braved the bad weather.

Soon the other two also appeared and she taught the class, who seemed much more relaxed this time, fed them Eccles cakes to great acclaim, and saw them on their way. As she was washing the dishes, she handled the knife she'd used on the cakes. She thought of the snowmobiler, his throat slashed, dying in the woods, and began to cry.

Crying brought on a spell of coughing. She made a coffee and sat on a rocking chair with it and her aunt's childish book. It was almost cat suppertime but she had a few minutes. She read "The Talking Dog," a story about a man who taught his dog to have a conversation with him. The man, a Mr. Leger, owned a candy store and gas station not far from Aunt Maggie's house and she'd been allowed to bike there alone or with her sister Mary or brother Gerald (Gerry's dad).

So, Maggie had been treated to many instances of Mr. Leger putting the dog, a small beagleish thing named Frisky, on a stool in the candy shop and engaging it in a chat, much to the delight of his customers, as it turned its nose upward and bayed.

Gerry fed the cats and heated up some of Prudence's good soup. Then she read "The Laughing Child." Almost immediately, she was riveted.

The ten-year-old author explained that her mother had told her this story so she'd understand why their neighbour lived in seclusion.

As soon as Gerry read, "I often look through the thicket at the big white house next door and wonder about the lady who lives there," she realized it was the now empty house her aunt was referring to and its lonely occupant must be the woman Gerry remembered from her own early childhood.

She heard a snowmobile's distinctive roar as it drove by her house. She tensed, but the roar continued past and faded as it made for Lovering. Not all snowmobilers are bad, she reminded herself with a shiver.

She continued to read "The Laughing Child," written in her aunt's childish scrawl. Simply told, it was the story of Helen Parsley, cousin to Maggie's grandmother, Elizabeth Parsley Coneybear. Helen married (Maggie didn't say to whom) and came to live near Elizabeth—in the house next door.

Elizabeth had a daughter—Mary Ann—and Helen had one also—Winnifred—and the two little girls played together. Then Helen had a son—Henry—when Winnifred was six years old. And, sadly, Winnifred was playing with the baby when she dropped him out the nursery window. He died. Winnifred became a recluse and lived with her parents until they died and after, alone.

Gerry consulted her family tree, under a pile of Mug drawings on the table, and saw that all this must have happened around 1890 or thereabouts. Helen was not on the tree but, of course, Elizabeth was. She followed her own line back to her great-grandmother Elizabeth, then dropped her gaze to her daughter Mary Anne, Winnifred's playmate. The first of four children. Born in 1893. "Oh," Gerry sighed. "Died 1915. Oh. Only twenty-two. How sad. And then her brother Alfred killed in the Great War in the same year. Their parents must have been crushed. And Winnifred must be the woman who lived to be more than 100, who's recently died.

"So that's the old lady I'd see creeping around the garden when I was little," Gerry told Bob, who, for once, had supplanted Min Min on her lap. "She was a distant relative. I guess if I live here long enough, a lot of things may be explained."

There was a little more to the story. The child Maggie wrote, "Sometimes when no one else is around I hear two little girls laughing and playing in the garden. And then I hear just one child laughing. And then the laughing turns to crying. I haven't told anyone about this but it's real. Mr. Puff hears it too. It makes his hair stand on end and he runs away."

Gerry drew a little diagram off to one side of the tree showing Helen, Winnifred and Henry, with a line connecting Helen to Elizabeth. Then she put the tree away, Aunt Maggie's storybook with it. She felt drained and listlessly opened her *Mug the Bug* file. Dangerously low. Work always distracts me, she thought. Time for Mug to meet some more cats.

Two strips and three hours later, she felt tired but much, much better.

# 16

"I found out about the child," Gerry said absently as Prudence carefully manoeuvred the Mini around a snowplow that was stopped at the bottom of her road. As this involved negotiating a three-way stop, one direction of which was blocked by the snowplow, Prudence was giving driving her full attention.

"Huh?"

"In the house next door. The one Mrs. Smith mentioned to you? I found a little book of stories Aunt Maggie put together when she was about ten. About local people and things she thought were interesting. Or stuff her mother told her. And there was a story about the child."

"Ah." Prudence tentatively braked, then drove through snowdrifts that had formed where the road was exposed to the lake wind.

"I thought I would paint a herd of polka-dotted hippopotamuses coming across the ice," Gerry said casually.

"It's hippopotami and that would be surrealism, wouldn't it?"

"Ah ha! So you are listening."

"I've got my hands full, in case you hadn't noticed!"

"Oh, you're fine. Easy on the brakes, slow turns, easy on the gas; you're doing it all right."

The snowplow, having seemingly resolved its difficulties, now roared up behind them and tailgated.

"Where does he expect me to go?" Prudence asked exasperatedly, looking in her rear-view mirror.

"The thing no driver can control: the other guy," Gerry reassured her. "Keep your nerve. We're almost home."

Prudence pulled into The Maples' side parking pad. The plow roared past, throwing a wave of snow and slush that hit the back of the Mini and almost filled the driveway, only recently cleaned by Gerry's contractors.

"What an asshole!" she stormed, exiting the car.

"Indeed," Prudence agreed. "Better shovel now so later you can leave for school not all in a sweat."

"I will. After breakfast. And I want you to read 'The Laughing Child' and tell me what you think."

They made coffee and Gerry ate toast with peanut butter. Then, with Bob supervising from the side-door steps, Gerry brushed mucky slush from the back of her car and shovelled the end of the driveway. When she came back in, Prudence had finished reading.

"What a surprise! I never knew Maggie wrote little stories like these. I remember she was good in English composition."

Gerry poured herself her second coffee of the day. "And?"

"And I know as much as you do. I didn't live at this end of Lovering when I was a child, remember? We'd visit but the house next door didn't register. And if the grown-ups weren't talking about it…"

"I guess it's the kind of family incident you would want to suppress, if you could," Gerry said slowly. "Winnifred—that's the child who dropped the baby—her best friend died young so she couldn't talk about it with her. And the grown-ups must have just closed ranks. And never referred to it again."

"But people knew, all the same," Prudence said wisely, "and Winnifred couldn't face the shame. When did she die?"

"Just recently, I believe."

"I came to work for Maggie in 1988 or thereabouts. She'd hurt her back and couldn't bend, so I started dropping by to do only the cat boxes at first, but as she got older she just couldn't be bothered with housework. So I took it on. I didn't pay much attention to the house next door and Maggie never mentioned anything about it. Or its inhabitant."

"Prudence, what did Mrs. Smith say about the child?"

"That it didn't mean it and that it was sorry."

"Aw. It sounds like that spirit wants to rest."

Prudence regarded Gerry with skepticism. "You sound as if you're buying into this whole spiritualism thing."

"Well, after our experience over Christmas...your experience, I mean. I believe in you, Prudence, so I have to suppose what you tell me is true. About the spirit world. And such." Gerry coughed.

"And how is the cold today?"

"Pretty done, I think. It's almost a week since I got it. Gosh! A week since the murder in the woods."

Prudence stood up. "I'm going to get cracking."

"And I'm going for a nice hot bath," Gerry said. "Going to steam away this cough."

After the last student stumbled through their presentation, Gerry gave a brief introduction to Impressionism.

"I have one word for you. Light. And one name. Monet. Claude Monet, 1840 to 1926. Your homework" (Groans, sighs and rustles as the students shifted.) "is to compare two paintings. *The Magpie*, painted in 1869, and *Green Reflections*, part of one of the panels that make up *Water Lilies*, done between 1920 and 1926. Talk about light, treatment of content and brushstrokes. I want five pages by Tuesday." (More groans.) "Come on, guys. If you start tonight, that's only a page—250 words—per day. Surprise me. Take your time and try to be original even as you reference other sources. Footnotes, please. This is a hand-in essay worth ten percent of your final mark so make it legible and good. That's it."

On her way home, remembering how she'd cried when drying Jay after the kitten had fallen into Gerry's bath, and how handling a kitchen knife had again made her cry, this time for Nolan Shrike and an unknown murdered snowmobiler, she had her eureka moment.

"Prudence! Prudence! You're not in a hurry, are you?"

Prudence wasn't, was rocking by the fire and had made a pot of chocolate coffee. "I hope you don't mind. I never tried that flavour before and I know you like a coffee around this time."

"Perfect. Perfect. I'll just heat some milk." Gerry scalded the milk on high in a small pot and frothed it with a little gizmo she had solely for that purpose. "Ah. Best time of the day."

"It is, isn't it?" Prudence agreed, as the two settled down in the living room, Bob on Gerry's lap, little Jay on Prudence's. "Your Eccles cakes came out just fine. I already ate two."

"Have another. I doubled the recipe so I have lots." They munched happily for a moment. "This morning in the bath I just let my mind go down one direction, then another. I had all this stuff in my head. Mr. Shrike looking after the house next door and being murdered there. Finding drugs in the woods. Snowmobiles. The dead snowmobiler.

"And those things were all mixed up with Graymalkin getting almost killed and me meeting Jean-Louis. And by the way, he hasn't called me since last weekend. So what's that all about?"

Prudence shrugged and made a face. "Go on."

"And then in the car this aft, it came to me. I had a good cry yesterday when I was washing the dishes. You know?"

Prudence nodded. "Lets the feelings out. You cried?"

"Well, it was pretty awful. The body, I mean. You couldn't see the face. The visor was down. So, except for the blood, it looked like a giant toy just sitting there."

Prudence patted Gerry's hand. "It will fade, the picture."

Gerry nodded. "Oh, I know. But today I realized. Prudence, a knife. Mr. Shrike and the guy in the woods were killed the same way. By a knife."

"It's a silent weapon," Prudence began.

"No, no. Don't you see? Same weapon. Maybe exactly the same weapon. Maybe the same murderer killed Nolan Shrike and the snowmobiler." She paused for effect. "The other snowmobiler!"

"The other snowmobiler?"

"There are always two!" Gerry said excitedly. "When I've been up in the woods! There were two last Friday night. J-L and I saw one heading for Lovering along the tracks and then we found the dead guy about a half hour later."

"So apart from dying by knife, what's Nolan Shrike got to do with anything?"

"Okay, okay. Snowmobiles in woods. Drugs in woods. Mrs. Shrike said her husband used to walk the dog in these woods. So all these things—snowmobiles, drugs and Shrike—in the woods."

"But he was killed next door," Prudence protested.

"Well, I often hear snowmobiles going by on Main Road, especially at night. Right by the house next door. So if we have Shrike and snowmobiles here, why not drugs?"

"There's something loose about your logic," Prudence said, shaking her head.

"That's where the knife or knives come in. Suppose we accept the snowmobiler in the woods was knifed there by another snowmobiler. Then it's possible Nolan Shrike was knifed by the same killer."

"And the one in the woods was killed because he knew about the Shrike killing, or knew and disapproved. And fell out with the killer!" Prudence was starting to get excited.

"Now you get it!" Gerry encouraged her.

Prudence wilted. "You know we're making it up, don't you?"

"No, no. We're feeling our way. We're intuiting," Gerry concluded.

"Huh." Prudence drained her coffee cup. "Well, I intuit I'm getting hungry so it's time for me to go home to my supper."

That evening Gerry cranked out another Mug episode and, taking her own advice so freely handed out to her art history students, planned out her weekend work schedule.

Friday she organized the next week's two lectures, thought about what the drawing class might do and finished two more Mugs by the time she settled down for her afternoon coffee. She flipped through Aunt Maggie's recipe collection. "Mm. Lemon cranberry scones. Mm. Got to be them." She started a shopping list with lemons and dried cranberries, and then checked supplies in the kitchen. "Rats, I'm out of everything again." She sat back down at the living room table.

"Okay, cats, shopping tomorrow. And I need to go to the bank. And Prudence wants to scrub out your cat boxes on Monday so I need tons of cat litter. And I want to drop in on Bea. Gosh, I better do some more Mug tonight. Tomorrow's going to be nothing but errands."

She worked until midnight, then stepped outside for a breath of fresh cold air, Jay tucked inside her coat, curious little face peeking out at this, her first winter.

"Look at the world, Jay. It's why we were born," Gerry urged the kitten, repeating words her mother had said to her when Gerry was a child. She often wondered if those instructions—look at the world—had been the reason she had become an artist. Gerry looked at the house next door. She pictured it in summer, surrounded by greenery; a happy young family of 100 years ago in residency.

She wondered if it had been summer the day Winnifred dropped Henry. Morning. If the nursery window had been open to admit the lake breeze. If a sheer curtain had wafted out of the room.

She walked down where there had been (until the last big snowfall) a path to the lake. The kitten, passive and warm inside her coat, purred.

She turned to face the backs of the houses. Her house shone with a few lights at one end: her porch, kitchen and living room were illuminated. Smoke from the fire exited the chimney. At the other end of the house, exhaust from the furnace did the same from its separate chimney. Her home looked snug and cozy. She turned her gaze to the right.

The uninhabited house slouched amidst the drifts of snow piled up by its walls. The semi-circular driveway that curved behind it hadn't been cleared.

Gerry thought she saw the shape of an animal flit across the house's backyard. She clutched Jay, thinking of the fisher that might be out hunting. The kitten mewed.

The shape on the lawn froze then continued on its intended trajectory away from where Gerry stood.

In the distance, she heard a snowmobile and, in her haste to re-enter her house, she missed the flicker of multi-coloured lights that briefly illuminated an upstairs window of the house next door, the echo of a child's sob.

# 17

Valentine's! How had this escaped her notice? Really? She was young, not unattractive, had a job (or ten) and owned her own house. And she was going to be alone on Valentine's Day. Again.

Gerry yanked one of the small grocery carts from where it nested with the others and turned left, began the clockwise stroll that was grocery shopping in Lovering. Because it was Saturday, the store was manned (and womanned) by the youth of Lovering, bored-looking young cashiers and bagboys.

"I bet they have dates, or parties to go to," Gerry muttered, flinging a less than satisfactory package of bacon back on the pile. "And I have work, work and more work, and a bunch of cats to go home to. Happy Valentine's." She found a package with the most meat and the least fat to satisfy her requirements and added it to her cart.

She zigged around a white-aproned, scared-looking kid, who was peering at best-before dates on packages of chicken before he deposited the rejects in a basket. Then she zagged right into Doug Shapland in front of the fish freezer. He deposited a large box of fish fingers in his big cart.

Gerry sneezed. She groped in her coat pocket for a gnarly tissue and blew. "Hi, Doug. Just finishing a cold."

He smiled. "Yeah, we've had it at our place. I didn't get it but the boys all did. Otherwise, we're good. How are you?"

Gerry, frantically hoping there was nothing disgusting smeared on her cheek or hanging out of her nose, tried to appear nonchalant. "Oh, very busy. Work, the cats, more work."

"I hear there've been some unfortunate events down your way." Doug lived at the other end of Lovering from Gerry, in a house he'd remodelled twenty years before.

"A body next door and one up in the woods." She lowered her voice. "And drugs."

His face darkened. "God, I hope none of my boys ever get involved in that. You want to move along and chat? Only, I've got to get back. I'm tending bar at the rink starting at one." The rink was the curling rink, indoors of course. Gerry was struck by the incongruity of Doug, a recovering alcoholic, tending bar, but supposed with the sailing club where he maintained boats closed, and gardens under snow, he had to take what jobs he could.

They entered the cookie and juice aisle and Doug loaded up. Gerry looked in dismay at his selections. She made a face. "Chocolate-covered marshmallow cookies? Really?"

He shrugged. "Geoff Jr.'s favourites. He gets them when he's ill." He added a few jugs of apple juice. "I swear they can each glug one of these a day."

Gerry looked thoughtful. "It's kind of like the cats. They don't do anything and they eat a lot."

Doug laughed as they strolled the soup aisle. Gerry took a couple of cans of chicken noodle. Doug chose six of a cheaper brand that was on sale and a flat of assorted Chinese noodle packs. Likewise, when they passed the canned fish. Gerry selected two tins of kippers; Doug got a six-pack of tuna.

"I'm beginning to see a pattern," she murmured. "You make me feel selfish."

"Oh, it's a reality check, having kids. It starts when they're born and you realize how helpless they are. And you can't help it. I couldn't anyway—apart from my addiction—I wanted to do everything for them. You'll see."

Gerry flushed, wondering how she'd ever get to the point of having children when she was alone on Valentine's. They'd reached the dairy aisle, and as she took her two-litre carton of milk, small sour cream and 300-gram package of cheese, she joked, “Don’t tell me: a sack of milk, a tub of yogurt and a giant cheese.”

Doug said nothing, just swung first one then another four-litre sack of milk into his cart, to which he added four four-packs of fruity yogurts and two immense slabs of cheese. “They each put about a cup of grated cheese on their pasta, besides eating tuna melts for in-between meal snacks.”

“Growing boys,” Gerry remarked respectfully, praying her future kids would include at least one girl. Then, as they passed the pasta and toilet paper and Doug continued to load his cart, she rather tactlessly blurted out, “Doug, however do you afford it?”

He froze and looked down at the cart. “Andrew has been very good. He used to give Margaret money. And now she’s not at home, he gives it to me. For the boys. He says, as he probably won’t have any kids, these are as close as he’s going to get.”

He looked so humble and dejected that Gerry felt her throat swell with emotion. This made her nose fill up and she had to use the wretched tissue again. In desperation, she reached for the closest box of tissues, tore it open and thankfully extracted two fresh tissues. She blew. Then, as if nothing had occurred, she selected her four bananas and two large oranges in silence as Doug chose two bunches of bananas, a bag of apples and another bag of the cheapest oranges.

Gerry moved ahead to the bread where she helped herself to a small artisanal loaf of cheese bread and her favourite croissants. Doug got two loaves of generic sliced whole wheat. As they approached the row of cash registers, Doug added a large heart-shaped box of Valentine’s chocolates. She wondered, were those for the boys? He motioned for Gerry to go first.

By now she was feeling totally awkward. She set the already opened box of tissues in front of the cashier who merely looked as if she'd seen it all before. She paid cash, waved and walked out of the store with her two bags of carefully curated comestibles. She put them in the Mini and blew her nose again. Now for the cat litter, she thought.

She was almost back at the store entrance, looking for a large grocery cart this time, when the automatic doors parted, revealing Doug brandishing the box of chocolates. "I thought you'd gone without saying goodbye," he said wildly.

"No, I just do the cat litter separately. That way I only have to push the heavy load straight to the cash. And not squish my food." She looked at the chocolates.

"These are for you," he said, handing them to her.

Her eyes filled with tears. "Oh, Doug," she began but he interrupted her.

"Argh! There's never any time! I've got half an hour to get this food home and be back in time for work." They gave each other a tentative kiss in the entranceway, other shoppers passing around them. Then, muttering, "later," he was gone.

Gerry pushed the cart to the cat litter section. Six boxes of the stuff were as much as she and the cart could handle. Not to mention her little car. She was thinking. Did he mean "later" as in, when the boys grow up and leave home? Or "later" as in, today, this weekend, this week?

The Mini was stuffed. "Well, at least I've forgotten about my cold for the last few minutes," she told herself, giving her nose a final tremendous blow. She looked in the mirror. The nose was red but the face looked happy. She eased the car onto Main Road and almost immediately had to brake. A car coming toward her had swerved into Gerry's lane to avoid a stream of snowmobilers driving at the side of the road. They were heading to the turnoff for the local bar.

"Bloody nuisances," she cursed, forgetting what excellent trails they made for snowshoers and skiers. A fine snow had begun to fall. She didn't feel ready yet for more solitude mitigated solely by the company of cats, so she headed over to Bea's.

As she walked up to the front door, she could hear some opera blaring even though the windows were all closed. She banged heavily on the front door. "Bea! Bea! Can you hear me?"

The door opened suddenly. Bea, a kitten perched on her shoulder, stood there grinning. From behind her, a soprano launched into song. The air smelled heavily of chocolate.

"I just thought I'd drop in. It's been a while. If you're busy—"

"Come in! Come in! Have some lunch. I've finished my Valentine's baking. Just got to ice and decorate later."

Gerry went in. "You're looking good," she told her friend. She'd forgotten how tall Bea was. Bea wasn't often out of her wheelchair.

"It must be a chocolate high. I've been snacking as I baked."

"Well, why don't I make the lunch while you and Cecilia rest?"

"It's pronounced *Chaycheelia*, Gerry. Get with the program," Bea requested, turning down the opera as they walked to the back of the house.

In the tiny conservatory, Bea's orchids flowered colourfully. En masse, Gerry found the pinks and mauves too much, but she had to admit, individual blooms were wonderful. Bea sat down and distracted the kitten with a plaid catnip mouse on the end of a long string. "I have to keep an eye on her or she trashes the plants."

Gerry teased. "How do you say it? Chinchillia?"

Bea snorted with laughter.

Gerry rummaged for bread and cheese and put it under the broiler while a can of cream of mushroom soup heated. "So what are you and Cece doing for Valentine's?"

"Oh, you know. Stay in and snuggle. Eat too much chocolate. Like that. You?"

Gerry brought the food to the kitchen table. Bea and Cecilia joined her. "Sing love songs to the cats?" she quipped. "Make nineteen heart-shaped servings of canned catfood?"

"What is wrong with the men around here?" Bea slurped her soup. "It must be winter. They'll all be holed up at home drinking beer in front of the hockey game."

"Ugh. I don't want one of those anyway. I want—" Here Gerry paused, not quite knowing what she wanted. She compromised with, "I met Doug at the grocery store and he gave me a box of chocolates. An impulse purchase. I guess he felt sorry for me."

"Well, I can see you're feeling sorry for you. How is he getting on? With the boys and everything?"

"He told me Andrew helps out financially."

Bea looked surprised, then nodded. "That makes sense. It was common knowledge your Uncle Geoff used to give Margaret money."

"Apparently Andrew did too. The boys are all sick with colds so Doug had to rush off. And he'll be working at the curling rink for the rest of the day."

"Sounds like he couldn't have asked you out even if he wanted to," Bea said shrewdly. "Us folks without kids don't realize how all-consuming they can be."

Gerry nodded. "I guess we're just at different stages of our lives—him getting the boys ready for the world, me still getting myself ready!" She sighed.

"What about Jean-Louis? Anything there?"

"I thought he might like me. But I still feel I'm missing something essential about him. When I was asleep at his place—"

"What? You didn't tell me you slept over!"

"No, no. When we, I, found the snowmobiler, after, the police questioned us at his place. I fell asleep on the couch. And I heard—"

"What? What? What did you hear?"

"It just seemed odd how familiar the cops seemed with him. With me it was all 'What did you do next, Miss Coneybear? Describe what you saw, please.' Stuff like that. But when they were talking to J-L, they were gruffer, seemed more upset with him."

"Do you think he's dealing drugs? On Royal Mountain?" Bea sounded excited.

Gerry made a face at her friend. "Next you're going to have him skiing down the mountain being chased by the Mounties. On reindeer." Gerry reflected. "No. I don't know what it is. He's just—off."

"Like old fish." Bea assumed a high-pitched British voice. "Duck's off. Sorry." When Gerry looked blank, she sighed. "I keep forgetting how young you are. Monty Python? *Fawlty Towers*? No? Nothing? God, your education has been neglected. Next time you're over, we'll watch something really, really funny."

"Don't say that. If I think it's supposed to be funny, I won't laugh. I'll be over-prepared or something. Anyway, I should go. I've got lots of stuff to unload from the car. Thank you for letting me make you lunch. No, don't get up. Happy Valentine's. And to Cece."

Gerry backed up out of the little parking space in front of Bea and Cece's townhouse. She felt cheered up, but then Bea always had that effect on her. Something to do with her "make the best of it and count your blessings" philosophy.

Gerry fiddled with the car radio, then looked up. "Cripes! Not again! Bad timing." Traffic had stopped in front of the bar as a stream of snowmobiles came onto the road. As she waited for them to cross to the snowy verge, Gerry looked at the bar.

A big old sprawling building, it reminded her of Cathy's bed and breakfast. But where Cathy's house was rambling and elegant, the bar was run down around the edges: its roof tiles curled and tattered; its veranda saggy. "An old drunk," Gerry said, "slouching in a beat-up old hat and baggy pants," and decided to draw a caricature of it when she got home.

The annoying machines had all crossed to her side of the road and were now dispersing. A few stayed by the roadside ahead of her and it was several minutes before she could safely pass them. She was almost at the tracks when something big, yellow and black roared in front of her car. She slammed on the brakes. "Bastard!" The snowmobile continued by the side of the tracks in the direction of Gerry's woods. She grew thoughtful, wondering if this was one of the two snowmobiles she'd previously seen or met there.

"And if the other guy is dead, this might be the murderer," she muttered, pulling into her driveway. She sat behind the wheel, staring at the lake. The afternoon had slipped away to be replaced by a winter's eve's brief twilight. She made her decision.

"Sorry, cats," she breathed, as she grabbed her snowshoes from the snowdrift where she had left them just outside the side door. "You'll just have to wait." She walked to Jean-Louis's driveway.

His car was there and smoke curled from the house's chimney. At his door, she hesitated. What if he wasn't to be trusted? What if he was a drug dealer? She put on the snowshoes and headed for the trail at the back of his house. Soon she found her rhythm. She reached the tracks by nightfall.

The railway disappeared into the distance to her left and her right, the thin tracks appearing insubstantial, even frail. She'd noticed before that once the ground was snow-covered, nights were never really dark. It was as if the snow soaked up light during the day only to give it back after dusk. No moon, no stars, just a blue-black clouded sky, whiteness below her feet, and the smudged shapes of the trees ahead.

Warm from her exertions, she unzipped her coat. She paused to listen for motors. The woods were still. Animals must be asleep. Or hunting. She shivered. Fox, wolves. They're more afraid of you than you are of them, she heard Prudence's voice saying.

She clumped down the path into the high woods where some of the oldest trees stood. And then she heard it: the distant roar of a snowmobile.

The sugar shack! She rushed off the path, sinking into unpacked snow, floundering. She made it around the back of the shack and waited, sweat turning cold on her body.

She zipped her jacket back up and crouched. The sound was coming from up the hill, from the pine plantation. She was right! The guy must have either dropped off or picked up another bag of drugs and was leaving the woods. Unless it was just some other snowmobiler enjoying a ride.

Gerry hoped she blended with the back of the building. The path zigzagged down the hill to her right and anyone looking at the shack in daylight would have had a clear view of her.

She saw him but couldn't tell if he saw her. Just before reaching the shack, and at the bottom of the hill, the snowmobiler cut his engine. Her snowshoe tracks! What if he looked this way? The tracks led right to where she was hunched.

She couldn't see him now. He was at the front of the shack. She heard the flick of a lighter and then a thin trickle of liquid hitting the snow. She grinned and felt an insane desire to laugh—or jump out and surprise him. He'd stopped for a cigarette and a piss.

If only she could edge around the side of the shack and see his face, she might be looking at Mr. Shrike's and the other snowmobiler's murderer! Bad idea, an inner voice warned. If he's killed two people, why wouldn't he make it three?

When he gunned his engine, she was tempted to move, but found she couldn't. She was freezing. And chicken. The machine headed toward the tracks. Gerry saw its tail lights as the path curved around to the left of the shack and watched with relief as the lights turned left again and roared away towards Lovering.

So if he picked up drugs, he's now gone to distribute them, she thought as she stretched and walked back onto the path. But if he was dropping off, then someone else will be coming to pick up the drugs, a local distributor. If I find the drugs and hide nearby, I can maybe see who that is. Okay.

Staying on the path the snowmobile had freshly packed down, and keeping alert for sounds of another machine, Gerry slowly climbed the hill.

Now she heard, or imagined she heard, little rustlings high in trees. She tried to go as quietly as possible, but the puffing sound of her own breath combining with the swoosh of her snowshoes meant she had to pause to listen.

By the time she'd climbed to where the pine trees in their stiff rows began, she was simultaneously hyperalert and physically exhausted. She had a fit of coughing as she entered the plantation.

It was dark. The pines, growing tightly together, blocked the night's light. Little snow had penetrated the canopy. In some places the pine-needled frozen ground was visible. And the temperature had dropped.

She undid the straps on her snowshoes and left them near the end of a row of trees. It was hard to see the witch's brooms at night. Gerry moved slowly down between the rows, pushing prickly boughs aside, looking up into the trees.

Was that—? No. That really was an animal's nest. Or a bird's. Here was a witch's broom, but it was empty. Absorbed in her task, she didn't notice the shadowy presence following her as she worked her way up one row, down another.

# 18

"She doesn't suspect a thing!" chortled Bea as Cece swung their Subaru wagon onto Gerry's parking pad next to her car.

"So we just say we felt sorry for her and brought some chocolate cupcakes and a few DVDs, right?"

"Right. And the others should be along in, oh, about fifteen minutes. They're all going to park up by the church hall and walk down. And Cathy's going to walk Blaise over from next door."

"So here goes," Cece announced and got out of the car. He crossed to help his wife and glanced down at the Mini. "That's funny. She hasn't unpacked her groceries. What time did she leave you?"

"Around four," Bea replied, grasping his hand. "Oh, you know Gerry. She probably went in, fed the cats and got absorbed in some drawing or other."

Cece hauled her to her feet and held her close. "You're full of beans today."

"I feel great," Bea admitted. They walked the few steps to The Maples' side entrance. Cece knocked. No answer. He peered in one of the kitchen windows.

"Nothing doing. The kitchen is dark and the door is closed. Stay here. I'm going around to the front." Every window he looked into indicated a dark and lifeless house. Except for the cats. Hearing human activity, hungry cats began jumping onto inside windowsills. It was seeing Bob parading back and forth on one such ledge and mewing pitifully that decided Cece.

"Something's wrong." He fumbled for his keys. (After confiscating duplicate keys to her house from various members of her family a few months previously, Gerry had thought it prudent to leave a spare set with her lawyer, as well as with Prudence.) "Gerry should be here and the cats are going crazy." He unlocked the side porch door then the kitchen door and ushered his wife in. She sat down on a kitchen stool.

"Suddenly I don't feel so full of beans," she said in a worried voice.

"I'm going to check the rest of the house," he said and opened the door to the living room. Instantly he was awash in a furry tide. "Help!" he yelped.

"Help yourself," said Bea, who was likewise inundated by a sea of hungry whiskered faces. "Go look for Gerry. She had a cold. Maybe she got worse and is in bed. I'll feed this bunch." She searched lower kitchen cupboards until she found a container of kibble. She dumped some into the empty tub under the table, first removing Jay who was sitting in it.

"I suspect," said Bea, "that you are still on just wet food, aren't you?" The kitten purred while the adult cats crunched and gobbled. In the fridge, Bea found an already opened can and fed the kitten in the sink, fending off greedy adults who, missing their wet ration, couldn't understand where their share might be.

By the time Cece returned, shaking his head, all had eaten enough and were dispersing back into the rest of the house. Bea was back on the stool with the kitten firmly ensconced on her lap. He announced, "She's not here. Could she be over at that fellow's place?"

"Maybe," Bea said doubtfully. "Maybe you better check." She waited as Cece went back outside, jogged up the road then returned.

"Nope. His car is there but he didn't answer the door."

Dark figures began to be visible loitering outside the kitchen entrance. "The others are starting to assemble," Bea said calmly. "Better let them in."

Cece admitted Cathy with Blaise. Behind them were Prudence and young Judith Parsley. David and Doug Shapland hurried onto the property. "You said to be prompt," Doug said breathlessly. "It was a rush but we're here."

They all crowded into the tiny kitchen. "She's not here," Cece said.

"What do you mean?" asked Prudence, putting a foil-covered pan on the counter. "Everyone just leave the food in here and go into the living room, for heaven's sake!"

Sheepishly, they did as they were told, divesting themselves of coats and hats and chattering about where Gerry could be. Blaise, Cathy, Judy, David and Bea all sat at the table. Doug and Cece stood irresolutely.

"What should we do?" Doug said quietly. "If she's not with any of us, where could she be?"

Bea, overhearing, said, "Well, you know Gerry and fast food. Maybe she went—oh, I'm so silly. Her car is here."

"Maybe she went for a ski. Or snowshoeing," Prudence suggested. "Doug, check the shed for her equipment." Doug took the shed keys from the hook by the door and went.

The others waited nervously. Cathy spoke up. "She's probably out with Jean-Louis. Maybe he asked her for a Valentine's supper."

Cece shook his head. "Nope. I checked. His car is there."

Doug returned. He nodded at Prudence. "Snowshoes are gone. But even if she decided to go, wouldn't she be back by now? It's not much fun up there after dark. If you're alone."

Cece interjected. "But that's just it. We don't know if she is or not."

Suddenly, a picture of Gerry either alone or accompanied by a possibly malevolent presence, in the woods where a murder had recently been committed, filled the minds of those gathered in her living room.

"I don't like it," said Doug. "I'm going up there. Which trails would she be likely to take?"

"From up behind my place," said Cathy eagerly. "The sugar shack trail. Go, Doug, but take someone with you."

"I'll come, Dad," David said.

Doug shook his head. "No, son. You haven't been well. Cece?"

Cece nodded and began to put on his coat. Bea made as if to stop him, checked herself and said in a low voice, "Don't overexert yourself, dear. You're not as young as you used to be."

He grinned wickedly. "Huh. I'm fitter than you think. Have to be, hauling you around, you great big woman." He gave her a loud kiss on one cheek. She smacked his shoulder.

"Flashlights," said Prudence, handing the two men one each. "Make sure you check the pine plantation," she added. After they'd left, she locked the door and put on the kettle.

Jean-Louis was tired. He'd had a long hard week since the murder in the woods. His bosses hadn't been well pleased about how he'd handled that. And, at the ski hill, his other bosses were becoming impatient with the amount of extra time he'd been taking off.

He rolled over on the couch. Harriet, asleep on the mat where a cool draft blew under the door, whined gently. His eyes snapped open. She was usually such a silent dog. She had to be, given the line of business in which he found himself. She whined again.

He sat up and looked blearily at the dog. "Hungry?" She wagged her tail. He filled her bowl, made himself a sandwich and stared morosely at the fire.

It was no good. He couldn't reconcile his life with Gerry's. She had the house with all the cats in it. She was making a life in Lovering, putting down roots. Whereas he...

Harriet had finished her meal and now stood at the door, head lowered, her curled tail slowly waving. "Want to pee?" He opened the door and watched as she relieved herself. He yawned. Harriet sniffed the snow in the driveway and on the lawn. She always sniffed the snow. Then he saw what she was sniffing, stiffened and took a few steps outside.

Snowshoe tracks, made by the wide old-fashioned ones he associated with Gerry, came up to the stoop, turned and headed into the field behind his cottage.

Had she come when he hadn't been home? But he'd been sleeping on the sofa since noon. If she'd knocked, he or Harriet for sure would have heard her. So she hadn't knocked. She'd decided to go into the woods alone. Why?

His eyes narrowed as his lips compressed. He made a phone call and went outside. He looked at the snowmobile. It would be fast. But skis would be quieter. He strapped them on, called the dog, and headed into the night.

Gerry's hand closed on the tightly wrapped parcel. "Gotcha!" she said softly, then looked around. All clear. She opened the bag and looked inside. Tablets, each enclosed in its little plastic cell. She rewrapped the parcel, put it in a pocket on the inside of her jacket and zipped both pocket and jacket closed.

She moved to the end of the row of pines towards the trail. As she stepped onto it she heard a sound coming from her left where the trail continued away from Lovering up toward the highway.

Suddenly Gerry wished she was not out in the woods alone and at night with who knew what type of drugs next to her body and who knew what kind of person or animal approaching. She looked up the trail. There, nose to the ground, was a dog. Or was it a wolf? A coyote? A coywolf? she thought hysterically, looking around for her snowshoes.

As the animal grew closer she saw it would every now and then lift its nose from the path and cast to either side. An experienced tracker, she thought, and recognized it.

Doug and Cece, one in his forties, the other a decade further along, walked moderately quickly along Main Road before turning up the well-plowed lane next to Cathy's property. They didn't speak.

Where Cathy's land ended and that belonging to the empty farmhouse ahead began, the snowplow had turned and they slowed, trudging through snow, in some places up over their knees. "Wait, Doug," gasped Cece. "There aren't any snowshoe tracks. Or ski tracks."

Doug stopped as Cece caught his breath. "I noticed that too," he said worriedly. "Shall we go on a bit or what?"

"I vote we go as far as the train tracks. If she was heading up to the woods, she'd have to cross them somewhere. We can fan out in either direction until we find her marks." Doug nodded and they continued.

It was with relief that they found a snowmobile path crossing the field surrounding the house. "Look!" Doug said, pointing downwards. Snowshoe tracks coming from the right led onto the trail.

"So she came from that fellow's cottage," said Cece, looking down. "I see cross-country ski tracks too. Over the snowshoes."

"So he was following her," said Doug. "By God, if he hurts her—"

"Calm down. Maybe they were together."

They doubled their speed, only sinking in a couple of inches. "Snowmobiles make good paths," panted Cece. "I'd forgotten that."

They reached the railroad. Evidence of snowmobiles went off in all directions but Gerry's tracks as well as the skier's had disappeared from the now bare icy path. Doug held up one hand. "Do you hear anything?"

Cece shook his head. "Now what?"

"She always talks about the sugar shack and the pine plantation Geoff planted. And that's the direction Cathy and Prudence suggested. Let's go that way first." They plunged down the little slope from the railway tracks, finding evidence of the skier but not of Gerry.

Doug flashed his light from side to side. "Here!" he called out, stepped off the path and fell into deep snow.

Cece flashed his light to the same spot. Snowshoe tracks led off behind the sugar shack, followed by the ski tracks. "Why would she—?" he began, but Doug held a finger to his lips.

He whispered. "I think we should be careful from now on. The tracks go behind the shack. She—or they—were hiding. I'm going to look."

Cece stayed on the path. Doug reappeared from around the far side of the shack and beckoned. Cece caught him up and saw the snowshoe tracks had also reappeared. As well as those of the skier.

They were halfway up when they heard a startled cry. They broke into a run. Cece slipped and fell, and watched as Doug continued up the hill and out of his view.

"No, no. It'll keep," Cathy said in a low voice to Prudence as they looked at the beef Wellington Cathy was unwrapping. "I just don't want it to get too cold in the fridge. Let's put it out here." She rewrapped the dough-encased meat and put it in the porch, on an old bureau on which was a basket of combs, brushes, scissors and nail clippers, Gerry's cat-grooming station.

"The vegs are ready to go. Whenever they get back." Prudence looked at Cathy who grimaced. If they got back, both seemed to be thinking.

Cathy the caterer spoke. "I think we should serve the crudités and cheeses. People are getting hungry." Prudence nodded and they prepared the appetizers.

When they carried them through to the living room, they found a strangely silent little group. Someone had started a fire. Blaise and Bea had the rockers by the fireplace; David and Judith were sitting on the hearthrug playing with Jay. Assorted cats paced around the edges of the room.

Judith looked at the cats uneasily. "They know we shouldn't be here without Gerry."

"Or they know something's happened to her," David said gloomily.

"I think it's just our worry transmitting to them," Prudence said kindly, handing around the raw veggies and dip. "No double dipping," she reminded.

Food calmed the cats wonderfully. They stopped agitating and closed in. "Don't feed them," warned Prudence. "That was Maggie's one rule. If you feed them once they'll come to expect it. And Gerry has to live with them."

"But they're so cute," Judith cooed as Jay arched her little back and rubbed along her leg.

"Graymalkin always gets a little from my plate," said Blaise, "and he's a perfect gentleman."

"Yes, but there's only one of him." Bea shuddered. "Can you imagine if all nineteen of these were hounding you while you ate? A nightmare." She leaned over to Blaise. "I confess, I feed my little Cecilia from my plate too."

The older people were sparing in what they ate but the younger ones made up for their lack of interest. "We better put some aside in a container for the others when they get back," Cathy cautioned quietly.

"Already done," Prudence said calmly.

Gerry's heart almost stopped when she saw the thin figure walking toward her.

"Miss Coneybear," said Elizabeth Shrike.

"Mrs. Shrike," Gerry replied, feeling as though they were acting like they were meeting at a formal occasion in the village instead of in the woods at night. "Beautiful evening. Walking the dog?"

The dog Sharp stood between the women for a moment, then resumed casting for a scent. He went down the row of pines from which Gerry had come. Both Gerry and Mrs. Shrike looked at the footprints he was following.

"My Uncle Geoff planted all these—" Gerry began.

Mrs. Shrike held up a hand. "Stop. Do you have something for me?"

The dog returned, following Gerry's tracks back to where she stood. He sat at her feet and looked up. On impulse, she reached out a hand to pet him. Her caress was accepted.

"Good dog. Good dog," she crooned. He sniffed her hand. She reached into a pocket and gave him a dog cookie. He ate it and then nosed out which pocket contained the drugs and sat again, close to that side. Gerry tried to appear nonchalant but must have looked nervous.

"He's not going to attack you," Mrs. Shrike said cuttingly. "He's a family pet."

"A family pet who's been trained to sniff out drugs," Gerry couldn't resist saying.

Mrs. Shrike flushed. "That was Nolan's idea. He'd worked in security and knew how easy it was to make stuff go missing. All it needs is one bent cop—" Her hand flew to her mouth.

"Ahh." The soft sound broke from Gerry's throat as various anomalies clicked into place. "You're not a killer, Mrs. Shrike," she said quietly.

Mrs. Shrike made a sound halfway between a sob and a hiccup. "No, but the people Nolan was working for are. They said if I didn't keep doing his work, I'd be next."

"Why did they kill him?"

“I persuaded Nolan to ‘burn’ the drugs, to take a bit off the side for ourselves to sell separately. To a local dealer. We needed the money. I needed the money. It hurts me to spend money and I can never get enough.” Glassy-eyed, Mrs. Shrike stared past Gerry’s shoulder as if she were reliving some experience that had turned her into a miser.

“Burn the drugs” sounded incongruous coming from the older woman’s mouth. Gerry put out a hand in what she hoped was a calming gesture. “That’s why you don’t eat and wear old clothes. And drive an ancient car,” she said softly. “I suppose you make the students work and take their money?”

“They’re young. Why shouldn’t they work?”

“They’re just kids,” Gerry protested. “And why would you threaten to kill them?”

“Not me! I was saying that their bosses would kill them if they were late. Don’t criticize me! Everything has been given to you!” Mrs. Shrike’s voice was becoming hysterical. The dog Sharp moved uneasily at her feet. “Don’t you think I feel bad? I’ve gotten two men killed! By the real boss.”

“I’m sorry,” Gerry said. “What do we do now?”

The silent watcher crept closer.

Jean-Louis skied as fast as he could, his brain furiously ticking. Ahead of him but not too far, Harriet—all business—tracked Gerry.

They reached the railway in record time. He took a minute to examine the snow in either direction along the line before following Harriet into the woods. The snowshoe tracks, visible starting from his backyard, had been obliterated by a fresh snowmobile trail. But had the vehicle been coming or going? It was a good thing he could rely on Harriet’s nose. He followed her into the woods.

He found and followed the snowshoe marks off the snowmobile trail to where they led to the sugar shack, pausing to listen carefully and draw a handgun from its holster.

He edged around the back of the shed. Nothing. She'd gotten off the trail to hide, obviously. From a snowmobiler?

He ran up the path that snaked between tall maple trees, thanking the job at Royal Mountain for his good conditioning and remembering how he'd coached Gerry to crawl up sideways, painful step by painful step. If she had gotten mixed up in this... His mouth set grimly. Collateral damage.

He reached the top of the hill and paused again, listening. Harriet came quietly at a hand gesture. She was really turning into a very good dog, he thought, and then heard a crack and a sudden cry.

Silently the watcher crept forward, focused on the two people and the dog. It decided to take the dog. But the bough on which it was crouched must have been rotten, and gave way under its slight weight, and the fisher found itself falling straight down, still clinging to the piece of wood.

The bough landed on the path between Gerry and Mrs. Shrike, breaking into several large pieces. The women screamed as the branch almost hit them and again when they saw part of it separate and shoot off into the pine plantation. The dog Sharp gave chase. Then another dog appeared and followed Sharp. Then a man skied up waving a gun. The women screamed again. Then another man appeared, running.

"Doug! Doug! He's got a gun!" yelled Gerry. She tackled Mrs. Shrike and lay on the ground, protecting the older woman.

Jean-Louis began to say, "Oh, so you're D—" when Doug plowed into him. The gun skidded into a snowdrift and out of sight.

"No! No! Stop!" Jean-Louis tried to defend himself but was hampered by his skis. Doug grabbed a chunk of wood and stood over him menacingly. Gerry and Mrs. Shrike got up slowly. Gerry scrabbled in the snow for Jean-Louis's gun. She didn't like to point it at him so handed it to Doug who had no such compunction. He dropped the chunk and covered Jean-Louis.

"Can I get up?" Jean-Louis asked.

Mrs. Shrike approached. "Who's he?"

Gerry turned to her in surprise. "Isn't he the one who's threatening you?"

Mrs. Shrike sniffed. "Never seen him before in my life."

And that's when Cece hobbled into view.

# 19

There ensued a confusion of snowmobiles converging on them from several directions, all manned by police.

Jean-Louis showed his identification, his gun was returned to him and Gerry sheepishly handed over the drugs. When she did, all he did was shake his head and cluck his tongue before turning his attention to Mrs. Shrike, who was taken away by snowmobile.

Cece, whose ankle was quite painful, was transported out on another. Which left Gerry, Doug and Jean-Louis facing each other.

"Wait!" Gerry said. "Her dog."

"Yes, where are the dogs?" Jean-Louis wondered. He whistled and waited.

The two dogs appeared, each with a scrap of fur in its mouth. Sharp had the head while a happy Harriet dropped the fisher's tail at her master's feet.

"Eew," said Gerry.

"I'll have it made into a hat. A souvenir of a successful bust. Or maybe I'll give it to you. For your birthday." He exchanged a look with Doug.

"No, thanks," Gerry said firmly. "The poor animal."

J-L shrugged. "Dogs are hunters too." He petted Sharp who had cast for Mrs. Shrike's scent, then given up. "I'll take this one. You say it's trained to sniff drugs, eh? Like Harriet."

"So Harriet's a police dog?" asked Gerry, scrunching the dog's ears affectionately.

"Almost," he said. "Well, we should be getting back. I'll have paperwork. And," he added grimly, "another matter to clear up."

"So J-L isn't the bad cop. His boss, his local boss, is. J-L was brought in as an unknown who could go undercover. And the bad cop thought J-L was investigating the small fry dealing on the ski hill, but really, he was trying to find out who on the local force was trafficking."

She munched happily, looking around at her friends seated in the formal dining room, at the flowers and candles and the remains of the good meal they'd all contributed to. "I never thought I'd like Brussels sprouts but I do. The way you prepare them, Prudence." She drank from her second glass of red wine. "And the beef, Cathy! You've outdone yourself!"

Cathy and Prudence exchanged an amused look. That Prudence's Brussels sprouts, steamed then lapped in a brown gravy infused with garlic, onion and thyme, and sprinkled with freshly toasted almond slivers, were good, was a given. As for the beef Wellington, better not to tell how, in the confusion of people coming and going, the kitchen door onto the porch had been left open. Fortunately, Cathy had been able to repair the pastry, gnawed by Bob and Ronald, after they'd clawed through the plastic wrap. After all, as Prudence had noted, it was going to be sterilized when it was cooked.

"He's had to sort all that out. He said he probably wouldn't be able to make it tonight."

Cathy and Prudence shared another look. Cathy shrugged. That her favourite, the exotic newcomer, had been elbowed out by the steadfast local, seemed indicated by Gerry's cheerfulness despite the former's absence. Prudence smiled and handed Doug another slice of beef.

Gerry looked at him. She warmed as she remembered how, after J-L had skied off with Sharp and Harriet—Harriet giving little longing looks of adoration at Gerry over her shoulder—Doug had grasped one of her hands, tucked it in his pocket and strode down the hill, her snowshoes under his arm. He hadn't said much but the action was enough.

Cece was receiving his own share of fond looks. Having refused to go to hospital, he'd made the first entrance, long before Doug and Gerry, leaning on a police officer in a snowmobile suit, and reassuring everyone that, yes, he was fine, just a sprain, and yes, Gerry and Doug were also fine and hadn't they better heat up the birthday girl's supper so it was ready when she arrived?

Bea was leaning against him. "Don't worry, dear," she reassured. "It will be my pleasure to wait on you for a change."

"Just need a pair of crutches and a pressure bandage," he replied gruffly.

Gerry took up the tale again. "There was never any danger. J-L knew he had his man as soon as Mrs. Shrike described him."

"But Doug didn't know that before," Prudence said quietly. "I think he was very brave."

"To Doug!" Cece toasted.

"To Doug!" everyone agreed.

"And to the birthday girl," Cece added.

"To Gerry!" all agreed.

"When do I get my presents?" she plaintively asked.

"After dessert," Prudence said severely, clearing away the dirty dishes. Cathy rose to help her.

"I wish Andrew could have been here," Gerry remarked idly.

"Oh. I heard from Markie today," Cathy replied. "They're having a wonderful time. And Andrew is coming back at the end of February."

"Well, I wish they could both be here," Gerry said, smiling at Cathy, who she knew missed her sister.

"Markie hinted they may both be here sooner than you think," Cathy said.

"Ooh!" crowed Bea. "More romance in the air."

Gerry sipped her wine and ventured a glance at Doug. He was frowning down at the table. "I don't see that there's any proof the police officer murdered the man in the woods or Mr. Shrike," he said.

Gerry shrugged. "Maybe J-L has evidence we don't know about. Or maybe Mrs. Shrike does. She knows he would meet her husband at the empty house. She can certainly link him to drug trafficking. That should be enough to put him away for a long, long time. Oh!"

Cathy had quietly been setting each place with a fresh plate, fork and spoon. Now Prudence had entered with a tiered pink cake plate on which were arranged many chocolate cupcakes, each with its own lit candle. This she set down in front of Gerry. A tub of ice cream and a can of whipped cream flanked the display.

"A cupcake tower!" said Bea, triumphantly. "I was just about to construct it when you showed up for lunch!"

"Was that today?" Gerry asked in an awe-struck voice. "I feel like I've lived a lifetime since then. Thank you so much. I've always wanted a cupcake tower."

"Of course you have. Now quit the chatting and serve them up!" Bea suggested.

"Make a wish!" David and Judith spoke simultaneously, looked at each other and laughed.

"Only twenty-seven candles," Blaise said. "Imagine being only twenty-seven!"

"One is for good luck," Bea explained. "Gerry's only twenty-six."

"Not yet," said Gerry, counting on her fingers as she energetically shook the whipped cream. "I'm twenty-five for another five days."

After she'd plopped a cupcake, a spoon of ice cream and a spurt of whipped cream on each plate, the presents appeared.

First Prudence pushed a squishy package at her. "For your outdoor adventures." A grey scarf with little cream pairs of crossed snowshoes on it was revealed.

"Oh, Prudence! You are clever! Thank you!"

From David was a print he'd made at school; five kittens playing on a rug. Gerry beamed "Lovely. I wonder where I'll hang it." David looked gratified.

Judith had bought three bars of homemade soap from a shop in the village: lavender, calendula-lemon and pine-scented. Blaise gave her a book of his poems; Doug two tickets to see a play at the local theatre. Cathy had made almond and apricot biscotti, dipped one end of each in dark chocolate and presented them in a large glass jar. The card read "With love from Cathy and Prince Charles." And Cece and Bea had gotten her two tickets to the same show as Doug had.

Bea removed the tickets after Gerry opened the envelope. "Never mind. I'll get you something else."

"How about an orchid?" Gerry requested.

"Done."

The friends dispersed around the house. Cathy and Prudence first cleared away the dessert dishes, then tidied the kitchen. Gerry, wandering from room to room, heard them laughing and Cathy say "you win!" and wondered what that was about.

She saw Blaise, asleep in a chair by the fire, and Judith, sitting in the chair next to him with Min Min on her lap. David, seated on the hearthrug, appeared to be sketching the scene. Mother, with Jay tucked close, dozed on the hearthrug near David.

The fire blazed cheerily. Other cats relaxed near the hearth. Bob, asleep on the mantel, opened one eye as Gerry chucked him under the chin. "I'll save you a nice bit of beef for later," she whispered, not knowing he'd already sampled it. He blinked one eye, as if to say, "knew I could count on you," and went back to sleep.

Gerry moved into the dining room where Cece and Bea, side by side, had propped their feet on a couple of chairs. Cats had drifted back into "their" room and retaken possession of the other dining chairs. Gerry drifted among them. "Hello, Cocoon. Hello, Harley. Hello, Max."

Cece and Bea each had a glass of wine and were toasting each other. Of course! Valentine's Day! And they'd chosen to spend it with her. Her throat ached (but whether for fondness of them or recognition of her own need, who's to say?) and she left them to it, closing the dining room door behind her.

She moved into the darkness of the large foyer and sat on the stairs leading up to the bedrooms. She wished—

"Gerry?" Doug let himself in from the back porch. He had fetched a bucket of firewood and a cold draft accompanied him. Gerry shivered. He put down the bucket and sat next to her. "Want me to get you your lovely new scarf?"

"No." She leaned and he took the hint, putting one arm around her.

"Gerry, I—"

"No," she repeated. "I know you have three sons. I know they're at a delicate age. I know you feel extra responsible for them because Uncle Geoff is gone and Margaret is—" She let the image of Doug's violent ex-wife dangle in the air. "I know only David likes me and I'd have to work to get James and Geoff Jr. to approve." His silence suddenly made her horribly afraid. "Or have I got it wrong?"

"Gerry—" A knock at the front door bewildered them both. They froze. The knock was repeated. "Damn!" Doug said, got up and let Jean-Louis in.

Jean-Louis gave him a brief look. "Hi." He turned to Gerry. "Gerry! I have to go back to the station but I wanted to drop off your gifts." Doug picked up the bucket of firewood and left the foyer. Gerry stood on the stairs.

"Finally, you're as tall as me," J-L joked and kissed her. He stepped back and handed her two packages.

Gerry held the gifts. "Come. Come through and meet the friends." She took him through the dining room, empty now except for cats, and into the living room where everyone was assembled. "Look," she said. "More presents."

Cathy brought J-L a slice of the Wellington, which he wolfed appreciatively. "Marry me!" he exclaimed and gave her a hug. Cathy looked like she wished he was serious.

Gerry opened the first gift—a bottle of red wine. "That was a fun night, eh, Gerry?" J-L said boisterously. "And, in memory of it—" She unwrapped the second flat object and stared, puzzled by it.

"A pizza stone!" exclaimed Cathy. "What a great present, Jean-Louis! I'll show you how to use it, Gerry."

Everyone else, who knew Gerry's penchant for take-out, ordering in, or just opening a can, instead of actually cooking a meal, smiled and agreed that it was, indeed, a great gift.

"Maybe Jean-Louis knows how to use a pizza stone," said Doug blandly.

J-L looked kindly at the older man. "Ah, but I'll be back in my home town this time tomorrow. Not that I won't have to return to testify in the future." He added, a trifle maliciously, "And court cases can drag on for years."

"Well, thank you very much for the gifts. And for showing me how to cross-country ski, especially how to go uphill." She kissed him on both cheeks.

The guests seemed to feel this was the signal to leave. Cathy helped Blaise with his coat, preparatory to accompanying him home.

"I'll give you a lift," Gerry said to Prudence.

"You'll do nothing of the sort," Cathy snorted. "It's your party. I'll be back soon and I'll take her. I haven't had a drink since seven-thirty," she added with a look in J-L's direction.

"And we'll get these two home," Doug said, indicating Cece and Bea. "David, you follow me in our car and I'll drive Cece's." And then, in front of everyone, he kissed Gerry quickly on the lips.

Judith left in her own vehicle. Jean-Louis walked back to his house after helping Cece and Bea into their car. Quicker than she would have thought possible, Gerry was alone with Prudence.

"Well," her friend said primly, "you have been going at it."

"You don't even know," Gerry said, her cheeks flushed, and helped herself to another cupcake with extra cream. "You don't even know."

Prudence smiled. "Tell me on Monday."

*Defiance licked his chops appreciatively. This pastry and meat combination was really rather clever.*

*He jumped down off the coffee table and sniffed the old man's leg. Motionless. The gentle snoring told him his friend had drifted off after their early supper. The frequency of the old man's naps led the sleek grey cat to suspect his friend might be turning into a cat. Any time was a good time for a nap. He was tempted to join him.*

*Instead he walked down the central hallway to the kitchen. He sniffed. The terrible smell was dissipating. Hours ago, his friend had switched on the oven at an extremely high heat and retreated into the living room with their supper, muttering, "There. That hasn't been done in years."*

*The terrible smell accompanied by acrid black smoke had ensued, and the old man had opened the sliding glass door in the kitchen, just a crack. It was this crack that Defiance was now inspecting.*

*The outside air wafting in smelled delicious. It had been a warmer day than usual, it seemed, and he could smell birds, trees and the cold tang of melting snow. He put his head into the crack and pushed. Nothing.*

*He turned and used a shoulder. Ow. That hurt his side. But he was determined. He stepped into the crack with one paw and pushed again. The door-window thing slid. He repeated the effort until he could fit his head. If his head fit, so would the rest of him. He pushed through, wincing as his scar pressed on the frame.*

*He knew he was forbidden to go outside—the old man was killing him with kindness—but therein lay the charm of it—being defiant.*

*He stepped onto the cool wet surface of his back patio and lifted his muzzle. No sour musky smell. He'd beat a swift retreat if he ever caught a whiff of that again. Perhaps the hunter had migrated. But there were always going to be others. He'd not relax his vigilance.*

*He padded the short distance to the gazebo where the old man liked to sit in summer, where they had in fact made their first real acquaintance. After the old woman had died and the new young one arrived to take her place. After he, Defiance, realized he could never fully relax with all those other cats around.*

*He looked towards the house of many cats. He might as well stroll over there, see if anyone he knew might be in a window.*

*He lowered himself under the gate and slowly walked the snowy path. Really, those women had been remiss. They hadn't shovelled for days. How was he supposed—*

*He froze, looking toward the house. His arch-enemy, the one the girl called Bob, the one who was now Top Cat since the old female calico had died, was curled up next to a lakeside window. He appeared to be sleeping.*

*Defiance crouched, his tail thrashing, then made a dash for the stone path, partially cleared, which paralleled the back wall of The Maples. In one fluid motion he leapt up into the window box and found himself in a miniature forest of cedar boughs someone had stuck into its soil. Good camouflage.*

*He crept slowly onto the window ledge, stretched up to his full length and tapped on the glass.*

*Hah! That had gotten a reaction. Bob, startled by activity coming from an unexpected direction, sat up and puffed his fur.*

*Defiance sat down, satisfied, and groomed his shoulder as Bob, meowing, agitated back and forth on the table on the other side of the glass.*

*Defiance groomed his crotch. Some of us, he seemed to indicate, are free to go out.*

*He crouched among the cedar boughs as he heard the young woman's voice say, "There's nothing there, Bob. Stop it! You're disturbing my papers!" She began to pull the curtains.*

*But as she did, he heard another voice, a man's, low and laughing, and saw the man who cut the grass in summer fold the girl in an embrace. The black and white cat sat and stared at Defiance, baffled.*

*Mission accomplished, Defiance leapt from the window box. He walked onto the parking pad, sat under the car and gazed at the empty house next door. His curiosity got the better of him and he jumped off the pad and into fairly deep snow.*

*The cold startled him. He breathed deeply a few times, which made his side hurt, but enabled him to bear the coldness. Hopping (like a wretched squirrel, he thought disgustedly), he made it to the thicket. The roughness and prickle of burr and thorn hurt his scar but he eased through and paused again, surveying the long low white house.*

*A tree creaked. Then another. He sniffed tiny footprints. Mice out foraging. He was tempted to follow the little tunnels they left on the surface of the snow. A mouse might be nice right about now. Then he heard a plaintive mew coming from the back of the house.*

*He approached cautiously. Something shifted at the level of the foundation. It moved only slightly and he strolled over to confront it.*

*The small female, black with white legs, was in a bad way. She was huddled into herself, shivering, and her eyes, gummy with discharge, barely opened to slits when she became aware of his presence. She crouched close to a small piece of wood that had been affixed low down to the house's wall.*

*He came close, and when she didn't react, sat at her side. Too bad she didn't have a cozy home with good food to which she could retreat. He sensed she didn't have long and an unfamiliar feeling entered him.*

*He left her and ran around to the side window. Why hadn't she gone in that way? Too weak? He jumped up onto the sill and pawed at the plywood there. Where before it had been absent or leaning, it now appeared to be firmly in place. Maybe she'd had another way in and that had also been blocked. He jumped back down and returned to the little cat. He would keep her company as she died.*

*He must have dozed off because he woke to find the other cat half underneath him. She seemed warmer and had ceased shivering. But what had woken him?*

*He blinked at the flickering lights reflected on the snow. Oh, that. He wasn't surprised when he heard first the window on the second storey above them slide up and then the child's laughter.*

*But tonight the child was more crying than laughing. It was annoying. It made the little female wake. She mewed.*

*Defiance sat up and looked across the icy surface of the lake. A mist was forming, coming closer. Low to the ice it swirled, elongated until it took the shape of a woman holding a misty baby. She swept over the ice onto the lawn and close to the two cats.*

*The cats' fur stood on end and both of them bristled, ears close to the skull, teeth bared.*

*But the wraith ignored them even as the upstairs lights twinkled and flashed until the whole backyard was awash in colour, and the laughing child's cries turned into moans, then whispers.*

*The woman held out her one free arm. The cats tensed. The child upstairs must have leapt out the window, for its silvery form flashed in front of the startled animals' eyes before it was caught by what they clearly realized could only be its mother. The coloured lights flared, then went out with a pop.*

*The three figures commingled into one vertical shape. It turned on its side and was just mist, floating out over the ice.*

*Defiance blinked. The feeling of the little female huddled close to him was not unpleasant. She mewed hungrily. He thought of the beef in pastry at home. Come on, he indicated by rising and brushing against her with his shoulder, you better come with me.*

# ABOUT THE BOOK

I'm indebted to *The History of Art* by Jacques Thuillier (Éditions Flammarion, Paris, 2003), from which I took the examples of paintings. The compare and contrast comments are mostly my own.

I'm also indebted to Terry O'Shaughnessy, director of The Greenwood Centre for Living History in Hudson, Quebec, the centuries-old house I use as a model for The Maples, who, mishearing the name of my dog Mata when I referred to her as a hairy husky, renamed her Harriet the husky, thus providing an idea for introducing such a one into *The Cat Between*. Terry and others at Greenwood, including Audrey Wall, have also graciously allowed me to hold launches for the Maples Mysteries at the house. And over the years, the local poetry group I belong to, the Greenwood Poets, have met there many times. Thank you!

When I wrote *The Cat Among Us*, the first in The Maples' series, my old cat Chanel, on whom Marigold the bossy calico is based, had just died, and the book became an homage to her.

In the second book, *The Cat Vanishes*, Bob, who's based on my other cat from that time, Aiden, assumes the dominant role, both in the book's action and in Gerry's heart. Sadly, Aiden has also left us.

Now in *The Cat Between* it's Stup—I mean Graymalkin's turn to give us the cat's eye view, and he's based on a cat that belonged to a landlady I lived with, in a long-ago life in Toronto. You could never completely trust him. A few new characters are introduced, not the least of whom are Harriet the husky, a.k.a. our husky-Labrador cross Mata, and Jay, based on my and my daughter's new kitten Jackie O.

That's why the first handwritten draft of this book is a bit more crumpled and tea-stained than previous ones: Jackie, sitting on my lap, and simultaneously playing with the curious dog Mata's nose as she learns her job of being a writer's cat.

## ABOUT THE AUTHOR

Born in Montreal and raised in Hudson, Quebec, Louise Carson studied music in Montreal and Toronto, played jazz piano and sang in the chorus of the Canadian Opera Company. Carson has published nine books: *Rope: A Tale Told in Prose and Verse*, set in eighteenth-century Scotland; *Mermaid Road*, a lyrical novella; *A Clearing*, a collection of poetry; *Executor*, a mystery set in China and Toronto; *In Which* and *Measured*: Books One and Two of her historical fantasy trilogy *The Chronicles of Deasil Widdy*; as well as her three Maples' mysteries: *The Cat Among Us, The Cat Vanishes* and *The Cat Between.*

Her poems appear in literary magazines, chapbooks and anthologies, including *The Best Canadian Poetry 2013*. She's been shortlisted in *FreeFall* magazine's annual contest three times and won a Manitoba Magazine Award. She has presented her work in many public forums in Montreal, Ottawa, Toronto, Saskatoon, Kingston and New York City.

She lives in St-Lazare, Quebec, where she writes, teaches music and gardens.

Eco-Audit
*Printing this book using Rolland Enviro 100 Book instead of virgin fibres paper saved the following resources:*

| Trees | Energy | Water | Air Emissions |
| --- | --- | --- | --- |
| 4 | 6 GJ | 1,000 L | 242 kg |